# THE UNEXPECTED
## *Package*

*Can an unexpected package change your life?*

The Unexpected Package
Book 3 in the Unexpected series

DL GALLIE

ROMANCE WITH A SHOT
OF SUSPENSE AND
A DASH OF COMEDY

Published by DL Gallie Author

First published 17th November 2019

Edited by Karen Hrdlicka, Barren Acres Editing

Cover Design by Dana Leah of Designs by Dana

❀ Created with Vellum

*Could an unexpected package change your life?*

My life hasn't exactly turned out as I planned, but I wouldn't change a thing. I have a great job. Fantastic friends and a love for coffee and wine; all that's missing is my happily ever after.

I haven't had the best of luck in the dating pool, and just when I think I'm destined to be alone, a package arrives, delivering me to Bennett Burnsteen.

Diving in head first, I give it my everything, but when Bennett's past comes back to claim what's now mine. I start to wonder if it this unexpected package was just a mistake after all.

## THE UNEXPECTED SERIES

THE UNEXPECTED SERIES
WHEN IT COMES TO LOVE, EXPECT THE UNEXPECTED

# ALSO BY DL GALLIE

## THE CASTAWAY GROVE COLLECTION

*Love has arrived in the Grove*

Oasis

Unequivocal Love

Five Words

Broken Rules - coming mid/late 2020

...and a few more as well.

---

## THE LIQUOR CABINET SERIES

*Liquor has never been so disturbingly saucy*

Malt Me (Book 1)

Tequila Healing (Book 2)

Wine Not (Book 3)

The Final Shot (Book 4)

The Liquor Cabinet: Series boxset

---

## STAND ALONES

Out of Nowhere

Antecedent

Seven Nights

Falling for Dr. Kelly, a Falling novel

Falling for Dr. Knight, a Falling novel - coming May 2020

Doc Steel - coming June 2020

The Dirty Dozen: Alpha edition

The Rule Breaker Anthology - coming soon

In the Dark of Night anthology (only available in paperback directly from me)

Titanic Tales, a charity anthology (no longer available)

Gone Coastal, a sizzling summer beach anthology (no longer available)

Leave Me Breathless: The Lilac Collection (no longer available)

*To Halle,*
*Thank you for being on my team*

# PROLOGUE

My name is Stacey Thomms. There was a point in my life when I realized I wanted what all my friends had. That special someone—who loved me unconditionally—two-point-five kids, and the white picket fence: the whole shebang.

One day, due to a delivery mix-up everything shifted. This package opened a door to a whole new chapter for me. Who knew one package had the power to change the course of my life?

This is the story of me and my unexpected package.

# CHAPTER 1

*...December 12th, 2019*

"SIGN HERE, PLEASE." THE YOUNG DELIVERY GUY'S VOICE BREAKS the silence in reception. His tone arrogant and the sassitude from him is on fire. He drops the clipboard onto my desk and stares at me in a 'hurry up, I got other shit to do' kind of way.

Shaking my head at the lil' punk's rudeness, I look down at the board but I don't see WFOX-FM listed. "Ummm, where did you need me to sign?"

"Line three," he huffs and rolls his eyes. *Asshole.*

Looking to line three, I notice it's not for us. "You are on the wrong floor, you want BKB Inc.—"

"Don't care, just sign or I return it to the depot as unde-liverable."

Shaking my head and rolling my eyes, I pick up my pen and scribble my signature. I normally wouldn't sign for something that isn't mine, but for some reason, I feel like I *need* to sign for this package. He dumps a box on my desk, picks up his clip-board, and turns to leave. The elevator doors open, and he shoves aside Kasey as she steps out.

"Watch where you're going, fatty," he snarls.

"Excuse me, what did you say, you little shithead?" Kasey snaps back, but the elevator doors close before she gets a reply.

"What a little asshole," Kasey mumbles to herself as she waddles over to me. "Hey, Stace."

"Asshole all right. The shithead made me sign for this." Pointing to the box, I confirm, "It's for the next floor up."

"Why?" Kasey asks, rubbing her lower back.

"'Cause, as you stated, he's an asshole shithead douchehole. You okay?"

"Yeah, my lower back is killing me. I'm so over being preg-nant." But I know she's lying, the smile on her face tells me otherwise, and if anyone deserves to be happy, it's Kasey. This year has been tough for Kase, but she's come out on top and I've never seen her looking happier than she is now. I feel like a bitch thinking that because she was happy with Kody, but with Bran-son, it's another level of happy. It's like she found that missing piece, and now she's on cloud nine million.

"I can't believe you are still working. You should be on maternity leave already. Sitting on the couch, eating that horrible stuff you can't get enough of, and watching *Days of our Lives*."

"Don't start, you sound like Branson, and it's the best food ever. Pretty sure I'll be fine, tomorrow is my last day and come next week, I'll be doing exactly what you said. But instead of that crap you watch, I'll be drooling over Sam and Dean."

"*Supernatural*, nice. I'll allow that amendment."

"Thanks."

"Any chance you'll amend the shit you eat?"

"Nope, that 'shit' as you so call it, is divine."

"Yeah, nah, not divine at all, Kase. With you gone, so will that nasty snow pea and salsa shit."

"You know, it feels like everyone is trying to get rid of me."

"Why would we want to do that, Buttercup?" Gage says, as he drops some envelopes in the outgoing mail pile.

A laugh escapes when I hear him call her Buttercup. "Dude, don't engage her," I say, as I notice Kase poke her tongue at our marketing manager, "she's hangry and the delivery ass just insulted her."

"I'll risk it, I have to get it in the jabs while I can," he nonchalantly says. He turns to Kase and places his arm around her shoulder. "This place won't be the same when you go on maternity leave."

"Pffft," she scoffs, "You won't miss me at all."

"We won't miss your snow pea and salsa obsession," Stacey interjects. "That shit is nastier than nasty."

"Is not," she scoffs in reply.

"Great comeback there, Buttercup, but Stace is right, that shit is nasty as fuck." Gage shudders as he says this.

Kasey pushes him away. "Fuck off, asshole," she snips. Flipping him the bird as she waddles down the hall toward her office.

Gage and I both laugh.

Standing up, I grab the mystery package, and place it on my desk, when I notice Gage lingering. "You all good?"

"Yeah, just realizing I really will miss her when she goes on maternity leave."

"Place definitely won't be the same without her," I sigh, "Do you think she'll be okay?"

"Yeah." He nods. "She has Branson."

"He does love her unconditionally," I say, wishing I had someone love me like Branson loves her. Sure, their relationship is a tad unconventional, considering he's her dead baby daddy's brother. But Kody, rest his soul, must have known something was going to happen to him because—from beyond the grave—he gave his blessing.

"You'll find someone," Gage says, bringing me back to the present.

"Huh?" I deadpan, confused at his statement.

"You'll find your one. Kasey found hers, twice, and I found mine. If a Grinch like me can, you will too."

"You've become Mr. Philosophical when it comes to love and shit. How do you do that? How do you know what I'm thinking?"

"Marlee. She brings out the best in me." With that statement, he turns and heads back to his office and as I watch him walk away from me, I wonder if he's right. Will I ever find my one true love?

My track record with men hasn't been the best. There was Jon, the unemployed accountant. Then there was Evan, the two-timing pin-dick. And the latest loser in the Stacey Thomms dating disaster folder was Gavin, the attorney. I really thought he was the one...but then he was arrested for withholding evidence and money laundering. Clearly I have great taste in men—not—maybe I should become a lesbian. Chicks are easier to manage and decipher. Nah, I love dick too much, so that's a firm no on becoming a lesbian. Maybe I'm destined to be alone due to something terrible I did in a past life, or as Mom keeps telling me, "Mr. Right will appear in the least likely way and when I least expect it." I really hope she's right. Shaking my head, I grab the delivery, and head up to BKB Incorporated to deliver their package.

Little did I know, this unexpected package was about to change my life.

# CHAPTER 2

WITH THE PACKAGE IN HAND, I WALK OVER TO THE ELEVATORS AND when the doors open, I step in and press the button for the next floor up. I should take the stairs since it's one floor, but these heels aren't really made for walking up a flight of stairs, so the elevator it is. Seconds later, the doors open and I step out into the reception of BKB. The guy behind the desk raises his finger in the "hang on a moment" motion and answers the phone "Welcome to BKB Incorporated, how may I assist you?"

He listens, rolls his eyes dramatically, and takes a message. After he hangs up, he looks to me and smiles. His smile is radiant, perfect for the first person you see when you enter a business. His eyes are a mesmerizing blue, and then he speaks and his voice isn't what I expected. It's deep and rough, yet gentle and calming. "Sorry to keep you, how can I help you?"

"Hey, I'm Stacey from WFOX-FM downstairs, this," I lift the box, "was delivered to us by mistake, and the delivery kid was a super asshole. So to save my sanity, and not murder the little douche punk, I signed for it."

His eyes drop to the package and his face lights up, "Oh my God, you are a lifesaver. If this package hadn't arrived for Bennett in the next three point five seconds, I was going to go change my name to Georgie, move to Australia, and live with the kangaroos."

I laugh at his response, but when I see the seriousness on his face, I stop mid-laugh. Before I can reply, a deep baritone voice bellows down the hall, "Has my package arrived yet?" accompanied by shoes clicking along the wooden floorboards.

Turning my head in the direction the voice came from, my mouth drops open when he steps into the reception area. The man before me is stunning—no—stunning isn't the right word; he is drop-fucking-dead-my-panties-just-disintegrated-gorgeous. He's got to be at least six and a half feet tall. Broad shoulders. Muscular arms are covered in sexy as sin tattoos, since his sleeves are folded to his elbows. Brown hair flops sexily onto his forehead. Piercing hazel green eyes that are a similar shade to mine. He stops mid-step when he sees me, and his eyes drop to the box in my hands. "Why do you have my package?"

My eyes drop to *his* package and I'm impressed with what I see hidden beneath his dress pants. Lifting my gaze to meet his again, I stop breathing when I notice his eyes roaming over my body. *Holy fuck, Stacey*, I think to myself as I continue to gaze at the man before me. Dropping my eyes from his intense stare, I smile when I realize what I'm wearing, ever so grateful I look smokin' hot today. I'm wearing a black pencil skirt, with a pale pink sleeveless blouse tucked in, just the right amount of cleavage on display—and a killer pair of pumps that showcase my legs—thank you StairMaster for giving me killer pins. The clearing of his throat snaps me back to the present.

"Sorry, what?" I reply like a dufus.

"My package, why do you have it?"

"It was delivered to us downstairs by mistake. The delivery boy was an ass. I signed for it so it wasn't retuned to the depot. I was just delivering it here to Blair." Looking to him, I smile when I see his shoulders relax.

"Stacey was being nice," Blair says. "You should try it sometime," he cheekily adds, garnering himself a murderous look from the man before me.

"Thank you," Mister Serious says, the deep timbre of his voice prickling my skin. He steps toward me and as he takes the box from my hand, our fingers brush, ever so lightly. A spark zaps through my body, my eyes widen in shock, and from the look on his face, he felt it too.

"You're welcome," I manage to squeak out, my eyes locked on the sexy as sin man before me. My throat suddenly dry and my panties soaked. *Get it together, Thomms*, I internally chastise myself. "I'm just glad to deliver such an important package."

"And I really appreciate it…" He stops and looks at me.

"Stacey, Stacey Thomms."

"Thanks you, Stacey. I'm Bennett."

He steps forward and offers me his hand. Placing mine in his, that jolt of electricity sparks between us once again. I inhale loudly as my body reacts to his touch. I've never had a reaction to a man like this before. Not wanting to break the connection—but knowing I must—otherwise it will become weird, and this moment is already surreal and out of this world, I let go of his hand. "And on that note, I'll see you around." Turning on my heel, I walk toward the elevator and press the call button.

The doors open, and just as I'm stepping in Mr. Sex-on-a-Stick, shouts, "Thank you again, Stacey, I appreciate it."

Looking over my shoulder, I smile and nod my head. The look he's giving me right now is smoldering. It's a stare right out of the hottest romance novel I have ever read. My heart rate increases as I stare at him. The elevator doors close, blocking him from view. Leaning against the sidewall, I lift my hand to my chest. My heart rapidly beating. "Holy fuck," I mumble to myself.

Stepping into reception at WFOX-FM, I walk toward my desk and sit down. My mind drifting to the man from upstairs; I wonder to myself if I will ever see him again.

# CHAPTER 3
# BENNETT

Staring at the clock on the wall, I become frustrated when I realize the package still has not arrived. I know I'm overreacting, but the item within this package is important. Pushing up from my desk, I storm out of my office and toward reception. My shoes echo on the wood floors, and I regret getting them now, the noise is annoying on a daily basis. "Has my package arrived yet?" I shout, louder than necessary but I really need, no want this package. I've been waiting for what feels like forever. As I step into reception, I pause mid-step. Standing before me is a goddess. A sexy as fuck woman. Black skirt, pink blouse, sexy as hell legs. A body to die for. My eyes roam over her body and my cock agrees. It twitches in my pants, pressing on my zipper as my eyes continue to take in the woman before me, and then I see it, my package.

Lifting my gaze to her face, I notice her eyes are on locked on me, and then I realize her eyes are eerily similar to mine. "Why do you have my package?" I ask, her eyes drop to *my* package—and not the one in her hands—but the one in my pants. She swallows deeply, and then she looks at me again and smirks, she totally just busted me checking her out.

Clearing my throat, her cheeks tinge pink with…embarrassment? Arousal? Both? That aside, we get to the issue of my package, the one in her hands, and I discover she works at WFOX-FM, one floor below. She hands the box to me and when our hands touch, fireworks explode through my body. I haven't felt a zap like that in a long time, not since 'she who shall not be named.'

She seems to be feeling what I'm feeling, she's just as flustered as I am. Not wanting her to leave, I ask for her name and when she places her hand in mine, again that spark ignites my body and soul. She says her goodbye and I watch her intently as she heads toward the elevators.

"Thank you again, I appreciate it," I say as she steps into the waiting car. She looks over her shoulder at me, and in this light, the green of her eyes pop. Again my cock comes to life, pressing firmer against my zipper. I'm ever so grateful to have this box in my hands right now.

With our eyes locked on one another, the doors close. Instantly, I feel the loss of her. Sighing, I turn to head back to my office and notice Blair staring at me. "Can I help you?" I ask.

The corner of his mouth lifts in a grin. "Ummm, what was that?"

"What was what?" I try to act coy, but I'm totally failing right now.

"That. There. The heat radiating between you two was off the charts."

"I don't know what you are referring to."

He eyes me suspiciously. "Don't play dumb with me, Burnsteen." He pauses and stares me down. "Are you going to go after her?"

I stare at him, contemplating his words, but after the distaste with you know who, I'm not sure I want to go there again. A look of recognition passes over his face and he shakes his head.

"Do not let that she-devil-whore stop you from moving on. She has," I shudder at his words, "you need to as well. Take a leap."

"Blair, I…I don't know."

"Dude, that woman there," he points to the elevator doors, "she wants you. You want her. Go for it."

"It's not that easy—"

"Don't," he snaps, "don't even finish that statement."

Not wanting to entertain this conversation any further, I start toward my office. "Get back to work."

With an eye roll and a shake of his head, Blair sits back down and grumbles to himself. Walking into my office, I place the box on my desk and sit back in my chair. Spinning around, I stare out the window; it's started to snow again. I love this time of year. Leaning back, I watch the flakes fall from the sky and my mind drifts to Stacey. I do want to get to know her, but I'm scared. The last time I gave my heart to someone, they stomped on it and obliterated me. I'm not sure I can handle that again.

My phone dings with a text. Picking it up, I shake my head when I read it.

**Blair:** *Take a leap.*

I roll my eyes at his text. Another one immediately comes through.

**Blair:** *Do it.*
**Blair:** *If you don't, I will. That chick is hawt.*

I growl when I read the last text.

**Bennett:** *Get back to work or you're fired.*
**Blair:** *You can't fire your business partner.*
**Bennett:** *No, but I can kill you and that solves two problems.*

A belly laugh from reception floats downs the hall and into my office. I can't help but grin. Throwing my phone onto my desk, I grab the box and carefully open it. Pulling out the book, I smile as my eyes rake over the stunning cover. This book is special: it's one of only twenty-six copies of Stephen King's *Firestarter* wrapped in a special aluminum-coated cloth jacket. Quite the pun, considering the premise of the story; a girl who starts fires with her mind. It's stunning and was totally worth the wait…and the price.

Placing the book on my desk, I flop into my chair and sigh when Blair's text repeats over and over in my mind: *Take a leap.* Then I make a decision, I decide, *What the hell.* I'm going to give it a try with Stacey…and I know just how I can see her again.

# CHAPTER 4

TODAY IS KASEY'S LAST DAY. I'M GOING TO MISS HER LIKE CRAZY. Her going away party has just wound up. I'm walking back to reception, and I notice the door to her office is closed. I'm a little sad she didn't say goodbye, but I know my best friend, she would have wanted a quiet escape. She's not one to be the center of attention.

Grabbing my handbag and coat, I head to the elevator, and when the doors open, I smile when I see Blair from upstairs inside. If I'm honest, I'm also a little sad that he isn't Bennett.

"Hey, stranger," he says with a smile as I step in.

"Stranger?" I question.

"Sounded good when I said it," he chuckles, shrugging his shoulders. We both laugh. "Big plans for the weekend?"

"Not really," I sadly say when I realize I have nothing planned. *I'm so boring.* "You?"

"Bennett and I are heading to the game this weekend at Soldier Field."

"Sounds fun." I have no idea who's even playing...or what they play there, but at the mention of Bennett, my mood perks up. "You two hang out a lot?"

"Yeah, we actually live on the same street. He and I have been friends since we were little kids. He's my brother from another mother."

"And you work together?"

He nods his head. "Yeah, I'm the only one who can put up with his shit," he laughs. "Actually, it's pretty great working with him. I'm proud of what we've achieved."

My eyes scrunch in confusion, "I thought...never mind." I don't want to offend the guy by insinuating he was the receptionist, but from the look on his face, he already knows what I was thinking.

"I know what you thought, but I'm actually a one-third partner of BKB with Bennett and our buddy, Keeton. I was filling in for our receptionist, Barb, she had an emergency arise and had to leave early."

"Ohh, hope all is okay," I say, not sure what else to say.

"Yeah, she's a tough bird...she has to be to put up with the three of us."

We both laugh and then it's silent, but not uncomfortable. "What exactly do you guys do at BKB Inc?"

"If I told you, I'd have to kill you," he jokes, I don't laugh at his corny joke but I do shake my head and smirk. Thankfully, he laughs at my reaction. "Bad jokes aside, we are a consulting firm.

We work with clients on strategy, planning, and problem-solving, and help them develop business skills and knowledge. Ranging from designing a business model or marketing plan, to determining which marketing techniques to use and how to use and implement them."

"Sounds riveting," I say.

"Actually, it's amazing. Each job is different from the last and no solution is the same. I love tackling the problems. Delving into the crux of the issue and coming up with the action plan, it's great."

"That actually does sound awesome. Better than just being a receptionist."

"Actually, without a great receptionist a company is doomed to fail. Don't underestimate yourself, Stacey," he says. The doors open and he steps to the side, letting me pass. We walk in silence toward the doors. "Have a great weekend," he bids when we step out onto the street,

"You too," I say, and I watch him walk to the street and a waiting tank of a car. When he opens the passenger door, I see Bennett behind the wheel. Our eyes meet, and just like yesterday, my body comes alive from his gaze. Blair waves and closes the door, I stand on the sidewalk and stare at the dark gray car as it pulls into traffic.

Walking toward the "L" my mind drifts to Bennett and his piercing green eyes. If I feel like this from a glance, what would it be like if we were naked? Skin to skin. Flesh slapping together as he drives himself in and out of me. *Holy hotness, Batman.*

Walking up the stairs to the platform, I grab my phone from my bag and call Mom and Dad. We say our hellos and catch up, and then Mom asks the question she always asks. "Are you seeing anyone?"

I shake my head. "No, still all on my lonesome." I don't

know why I don't tell her there *is* someone who I would like to date. I vaguely listen to Mom and Dad, but my mind is on Bennett. I *really* want to date him, but I'm not sure he wants to date me.

We chat for a few more minutes and just as we say our good-byes, my train arrives. Hopping on, I take my seat and once again, my mind drifts again to Bennett. That man has overtaken my mind, just the thought of him sets my body ablaze.

When we reach my stop, I race home, I run myself a bath, grab a bottle of wine, my vibrator, and I get myself off to visions of Bennett and me together. Sadly, I admit to myself, it's the most intense orgasm I've had in months. Climbing into bed, I snuggle into my blankets and my last thought before I drift off to sleep is of Bennett and I ravaging each other in my bed.

# CHAPTER 5

*...December 31st, 2019*

Walking into Bin 501, I sigh when I realize, once again, I'll be ringing in the new year alone. Maybe next year, I tell myself as I take off my coat. Immediately, I spot Kasey, Branson, and KJ and head toward them. "Kasey," I say.

She smiles at me and steps toward me. Giving me a one-armed hug since she has her gorgeous baby boy in her arms. Her last day at work, when I thought she'd snuck away, she was actually asleep in her office. She got caught in the blizzard that night and went into labor, trapped in the office. Branson managed to arrive just in time and he delivered the baby. She gave birth Kody Gage Holmes, or KJ for short. Looking at the bundle of joy in her arms, I smile. "Kase, he's beautiful."

"He sure is." She beams.

"As is his mommy," Branson says, placing a kiss on her temple.

Once again, I find myself pining for a love like that. Excusing myself, I head toward the bar and order a glass of pinot noir. With my drink in hand, I turn around and bump into someone, spilling the red wine all over their crisp white shirt. Lifting my gaze from the stain, I stare up at the person and my mouth drops open in shock. "Bennett, shit. I'm so sorry."

"It's fine," he says, his gaze locked on mine.

We stare at one another.

Everything around me fades away; it's just us.

We continue to gaze at one another, ignoring everyone around us.

I'm mesmerized by his eyes, the carnal hunger reflecting in them.

My heart rapidly beats as I take in the man before me.

Someone bumps into me on their way to the bar, snapping me back to the present. Shaking my head, I clear my throat. "I'm so sorry. Send me the shirt and I'll have it laundered for you."

"Really, it's fine," he says, as he takes my now empty glass and places it on the bar behind me. "Two more, please," he asks the bartender, pressing me back into the wooden bar. Our bodies are inches apart. The heat surrounding us increases by a million degrees. I can see his pulse beating in his neck. A sudden urge to lean forward and lick it crosses my mind. Before I do something stupid, the barman passes Bennett two glasses of wine and he offers me one. Reaching out, I take the glass from him. He doesn't let go straight away. I don't want him to let go. Eventually he does and I feel the loss of his closeness.

Grabbing my elbow, he ushers me away from the chaos of the bar area. We find an empty high-top in the corner. He pulls out a chair for me and he helps me up onto the stool. His eyes dropping to my legs, I'm ever so glad I decided to wear a dress this evening. His gaze leaves my skin tingling.

Taking the stool across from me, we stare at one another. It's suddenly warm in here, and it's not from the red wine. Our moment is interrupted when Blair and another guy stop at the table, dropping a bottle of red and three glasses to the table.

"Dude, what happened to your shirt?" the other guy asks. Bennett flicks his head toward me and both of them look to me.

"Stacey," Blair says when he notices it's me. "What are you doing here?"

"Hey, Blair, I'm friends with the owner. What about you?"

"This guy," he points to the guy he's with, "met Branson a few weeks ago."

"Small world," I say, as I lift my wine and take a sip. My eyes dip closed as I enjoy my mouthful. A moan slips free as the robust cherry flavor dances on my taste buds.

"It's good, hey?" the stranger asks me. I nod my head in reply, a little embarrassed from my moment with the wine. "By the way, I'm Keeton," he says, offering me his hand.

"Stacey," I offer in return, as I take his outstretched hand. He brings my hand to his lips and places a kiss on my knuckles. Bennett growls from beside him. Keeton winks at me as he lets go of my hand, snickering at Bennett.

Blair laughs. "Down, boys," he says, and both Keeton and Bennett roll their eyes at him.

The four of us fall into easy conversation. We discuss different wines and I discover Bennett and I have a similar taste when it comes to wine. He tells me about a great winery, Acquaviva in Maple Park, which is only an hour away. He offers to take me their sometime. I know it was probably said in jest, but either way, it's nice to feel wanted.

Keeton and Blair disappear. It's just Bennett and me. I finish my wine and as I place my glass on the table, Bennett asks, "Would you like to dance?"

"I'd love to," I quickly reply. He stands up and offers me his hand. Placing my hand in his, I stand up and when I do, I stumble into his chest: his rock-hard, oh-so-fine chest. My hand lands on the wine stain. "I really am sorry about that."

"It's fine," he says. As he links his fingers with mine and leads us to the dance floor. Spinning me around, he pulls me toward him. He places his hand on my lower back and brings our joined hand between us. The heat emanating between us is palpable. I wrap my free arm around him and rest my head on his shoulder. For the first time in my life, my height is an advantage. We fit together perfectly. We sway in sync and lose ourselves to the music.

Our hands gently caress one another. We don't say a word but with our movements and bodies, we say everything we need. Even though we are dancing amongst one hundred other people, I feel like I'm the center of this man's world. We hardly know one another, but the connection I feel with him is stronger than I have ever felt before.

The song changes a few times but I don't notice what's playing. I'm lost in this moment with Bennett; it's perfect in every possible way. The song changes to an upbeat one, Bennett spins me out and pulls me back in. His eyes are boring into me and we continue to move with the music. It changes to a slow song again, and our bodies gravitate closer together. Our breathing mingles as I stare into his eyes, he leans forward to kiss me when suddenly, the countdown to the new year begins. Bennett and I stay in each other's embrace. Our breathing labored. Our bodies pressed together. Our eyes locked on one another. We stare at each other as everyone around us counts down until midnight and the new year.

3…

2…

1…

"Happy New Year!" everyone shouts around us.

We are frozen, staring at one another, until Bennett lifts his hands, grips my cheeks in his palms, and lowers his head toward me. My eyes close when I feel his lips on mine. Gripping his cheeks, I kiss him back. His tongue slides into my mouth. My tongue slips into his. My hands snake around his neck and I pull him into me. Deepening the kiss and connection between us.

Pulling back, he rests his forehead against mine. Breathing deeply. "Happy New Year, Stacey," he pants.

"Happy New Year, Bennett."

Placing my lips on his again, we kiss in the middle of the dance floor, oblivious to what's going on around us. It feels like it's just the two of us and I could not be happier. Even though I went home alone that night, it seems 2020 is off to a great start.

# CHAPTER 6

*...January 14th, 2020*

THIS LITTLE SHITHEAD FROM THE COURIER COMPANY IS REALLY starting to piss me off. This is the third time in the last two weeks he's delivered a package for BKB here. Each and every time, he doesn't give a shit that it's to the wrong floor, or company. The only good thing about it is I get to see Bennett when I deliver it. He always happens to be in reception when I pop up to deliver the package. It's almost like he knows it's coming. And each time, Barb is nowhere to be seen, I'm starting to think there is no Barb at all.

Today when I step out of the elevator, I'm met with an older woman. She smiles at me and it's bright, it lights up her face. "You must be the elusive, Barb," I say as I walk toward her.

"Yes I am." She beams. "And you are?"

"I'm Stacey from WFOX-FM. The delivery twat keeps dropping a package to us that's for Bennett."

She nods but doesn't say anything, before we can continue our conversation, the hairs on my neck stand on end and turning the corner is the man in question. He notices the box in my hand. "Again?"

Nodding my head, my eyes roam over his body. Man, this guy can rock a suit. Suits are to women, what lingerie is to men. *Sooo damn sexy.* He takes the final steps to me and plucks the box from my hands, placing it on Barb's desk. His smell envelops me and I breath him in. Closing my eyes briefly, I drift off to my sexy place with Bennett.

My eyes open again and I see Bennett hungrily staring at me. I lick my bottom lip and his eyes drop to my mouth, lifting my gaze to his, memories of our New Year's Eve kiss come back to me. My breath hitches in my throat, thankfully, the moment is interrupted when Barb says, "I'll call the delivery company today and tell them this is unacceptable." Her voice has a different pitch to earlier and the grin she throws at Bennett seems odd.

Bennett scowls at her. "It's fine, Barb, I'll do it."

A look passes between the two of them that leaves me stumped.

"Fine," Barb huffs, I'm clearly missing something here. "It was lovely to meet you, dear," she says, as she takes the box from Bennett and walks down the hallway, leaving the two of us alone. The air sizzling around us.

Breaking the silence, he asks, "Can I take you to dinn–" but before he can finish his question, the elevator doors open and a woman steps into reception. Bennett's eyes widen in surprise, with a hint of anger, and his demeanor turns to annoyance.

"Bennett, darling," the woman singsongs, as she walks over to him. She places her hands on his arms—*mine* I internally growl—and leans in for air kisses. He's frozen. Eyes locked on mine. The woman pulls back and follows his gaze. She stares me down, the look she throws my way is like I'm a piece of crap on her shoe. "Ohh, I'm sorry, am I interrupting?"

"Yes," Bennet replies, as I shake my head and say, "No."

Before anything else is said, I quickly jump into the elevator that Stuck-up Barbie just exited from. Leaning against the side-wall, I deflate at the thought of him with her. Seems like, once again, I picked a cheating ass to hook up with on New Year's Eve. Looks as if 2020 isn't off to a great start after all.

# CHAPTER 7

THE NEXT MORNING, THE DELIVERY TWAT ARRIVES, ONCE AGAIN, with a package for BKB. Just like each time, he doesn't give a crap he's on the wrong floor, and he's a rude, arrogant little shit. He even left one for the IT company located on three. Today I'm still cranky after discovering yesterday Bennett has a girlfriend. So when I see the delivery guy, I'm quite rude to him, but the little shithead just shrugs his shoulders. This time, he leaves without me signing for the delivery, he just dumps it on my desk and leaves.

Since I'm pissed off at Bennett and his cheating ass, I put the package to the side and finish sorting the mail, his precious package can wait. He doesn't deserve for me to drop everything for his stupid cheating sexy ass. Everyone must sense I'm in a mood because they smile, and then make a beeline for their office, not stopping to chat like they usually do.

A few hours later, the elevator dings and as soon as the doors open, my skin prickles and that tingly feeling washes over me. Sure enough, the cause of my mood steps into reception. Looking to him, I smile but it's not my normal cheerful one. "Welcome to WFOX-FM, how can I help you?"

"Stacey," he says. Just hearing his voice, chips away at the anger I have for him and then I remember Stuck-up Barbie and that chip falls back into place.

"Can I help you?" I snap. I know I'm not being professional right now but I'm pissed off, I think I deserve to be angry.

"I wanted to see if you wanted to have dinner with me? I didn't get to ask you yesterday before—"

"No," I snap. "I do not want to have dinner, or anything with you."

"Can I ask why?"

"Stuck-up Barbie," I snarkily reply.

"Who?" he asks, his face scrunching in confusion.

"The woman yesterday. Your girlfriend." His eyes pop open at what I'm saying. "I've been on the receiving end of a cheating ass." Standing up, I lean on my desk and glare at him. "I will NE-VER," I enunciate each part of the word with vehemence, "be the cheat-EE with the cheat-ER." Sitting down, I quietly add, "Why are men such assholes?"

He leans down on my desk now. His arms bulging at the pressure. *Stop checking him out*, I chastise myself. "Number one, I'm not a cheater. Never have cheated and never will. Anyone who does is a dog. Number two; she is NOT my girlfriend. She is

NOTHING to me anymore. And number three, I'm super hot for this sassy, smart-mouthed, sexy as fuck receptionist."

Staring up at him, my mouth drops open at his words. It opens and closes a few times, I don't know what to say. I feel like a total bitch for how I reacted, but I'm a woman. I don't think rationally at the best of times. Enter in a sexy-ass man and poof, rationale goneski.

"Well?" he questions.

Not wanting to admit defeat, I smirk. "Barb is a lucky woman to have you think so highly of her," I playfully reply.

"Okay, let me rephrase point number three. I'm super hot for this sassy, smart-mouthed, sexy as fuck receptionist, who works one floor down from my office. This woman has been at the forefront of my mind since we shared a kiss on New Year's Eve." He pauses. "Actually, she's been on my mind since she delivered a package to me thirty-three days ago."

"Ohh, her," I say, "Well, I can put in a good word with her, if you like? She and I are pretty tight."

"Please do," he says, "I'd really like to take her out to dinner this Friday night."

"I'm pretty sure I can get her to agree to that. But there's one condition."

"Name it. I'll do it."

"You need to kiss her like you did on New Year's Eve."

"With pleasure," he says, stepping around the desk. He leans down, grips my cheeks, and presses his lips to mine. His tongue seeks access to mouth and I willingly open. He slides it in and fucks my mouth with his tongue. Sliding my hands up into his hair, I kiss him back with everything I have. His kisses are much better than I remember, and it's only been fifteen days since I kissed him last.

Breaking the connection, I pant, "Yes. Yes, she will go out with you on Friday."

"Good," he says. He kisses me on the tip of my nose and walks back to the elevator, the doors open before he pushes the call button. Marlee steps out, and checks him out, as he steps in.

"You forgot your package!" I shout, as I stand up and point to the box sitting on my desk.

"You better deliver it then." He winks at me, just before the doors close and I notice he's grinning like the cat who caught the canary.

Dropping back to my seat, I shake my head at the turnabout of events. Lifting my hand to my lips, I run my finger across the bottom one. My plump, just been kissed, bottom lip is still tingling from our kiss, which is just as amazing as I remember.

"You okay, Stace?" Marlee asks me.

Nodding my head. "Mmmhmpf," I reply, with a goofy grin on my face.

"You sure? You look flushed. Are you getting sick?" she questions.

Shaking my head, I look at her. "No, really, I'm fine. I just... never mind. What are you doing here?" I look to her and then add, "WOW, you look hot today."

She smiles at me, her cheeks tinging pink. "Thanks. Just popping in to see my sexy man. It always feels weird in the new year not coming here daily. Don't get me wrong, I'm glad the toy drive is over, but I miss seeing you all on a daily basis."

"Yeah, I miss seeing you too. And now that Kase is on maternity leave and Chelle is still working from home, it's so quiet here."

"We need a girls' day."

"Yes, we do. I'm going to arrange something for this weekend."

"I'm free Sunday," she offers.

"Sunday it is then."

With a wave, she wanders off to see Gage and I sit back in my chair and spin around in glee. When my eyes land on the box, a smile breaks free. Who knew, a misdelivered package could bring so much excitement into my life.

# CHAPTER 8

...January 17th, 2020

IT'S FINALLY FRIDAY, THAT MEANS IT'S DATE DAY. I'M EXCITED AND, at the same time, nervous like you would not believe. I've just returned from lunch and I see a new delivery guy, with a box I'm getting to know quite well.

"Really, again?" I ask.

He looks questionably at me.

"Let me guess, you don't care that it's the wrong floor. Just sign on line blah blah or you'll return it to the depot?"

"Ummm….some guy just paid me fifty bucks to deliver this here."

"What?" I ask in shock, my voice an octave higher than usual.

His eyes bug wide open. "Ummm, ahh," he stammers, "just forget I said that."

"No, I don't think so, mister. Tell me exactly what's going on."

"Shit." I give him my best evil eye, "Fine," he huffs, "I was walking through the lobby and some guy stopped me and offered me a fifty to deliver this here."

"And you said yes, even though the label is clearly marked for the next floor up?"

"Lady, he offered *fifty* bucks." He places emphasis on the word fifty.

Shaking my head, I smile when I realize the effort Bennett has been going to in order to see me every couple of days. "Where do I sign?"

"Technically, I don't need you to as it's not an official delivery. But if you want to give me your number, that would be cool."

"Yeah, I don't think so, buddy. Just give me my package."

"Whatever," he says, throwing the box onto my desk. The office phone rings, so I quickly answer it and after transferring the call, I grab the box and take it up to Bennett.

Unsurprisingly, when I step out of the elevator, Bennett is waiting to me. "The jig's up, mister," I say, as I walk toward him.

"Huh?"

"Don't play dumb."

"I don't know what you mean," he playfully says.

Shoving the box at him, I question, "Really?"

"Really, really."

"Do not Donkey from *Shrek* me. I know you've been paying that punk little shit to incorrectly deliver this to me 'by accident.'" I air quote those two words, "Just so you can see me."

He places the box on the reception desk and stares me down. "Yeah, and?" *Huh, he didn't deny that.* The look he's giving me right now is carnal and definitely not suitable for work. I get the urge to throw myself at him and ravage him, right here in the reception area.

"You could have saved the effort and just come and talked to me...like a normal person would."

"Yeah, I'm not normal," he confirms with a grin, "besides; if I did that, I couldn't watch your ass as you walk away."

Shaking my head, I smile. "You are terrible."

"You cannot tell me it hasn't been a pleasure coming to see me these last few weeks."

"I plead the Fifth. And on that note, I'll be going."

Walking backward to the elevator, I lift my eyebrows and smirk in a "ha-ha, you can't see my ass" way.

"Are you going to deny me your ass?"

"In every sense of that statement, yes. No ass for you."

He pouts at me and I can't help but laugh. The doors open behind me, before I step in; I turn around, bend over, and shake my ass at him.

A groan emanates through the reception area of BKB Incorporated. *Score one for me,* I think as I step into the elevator. As the doors close, I turn to face him and blow him a kiss, giving him a little wave. As the car takes me down one level, I smirk to myself. I cannot wait for our date this evening.

# CHAPTER 9
# BENNETT

WHEN STACEY BENT OVER AND SHOOK HER ASS AT ME, IT TOOK every ounce of effort to not race over to her, throw her over my shoulder, stalk back to my office, and fuck the sass right out of her. This woman is driving me crazy in the sexiest way. I haven't felt like this about a woman in a very long time, not since Amity Cuthell. And nearly twelve months later, she's still causing havoc in my life. How I was ever in love with that she-devil still boggles my mind. She is evil incarnate; she literally is the devil in Prada; and not the fun Meryl Streep kind. The kind that scares young children and makes you want to run away and hide. She makes Lucifer look like the sweet angel he once was.

She almost cost me Stacey, and I cannot have that happen. I will not let that happen. Stacey has lit a spark inside of me that has been missing, and if I'm honest, I need to get to know this woman like I need my next breath.

I still can't believe she gave me a chance after Amity's game the other day. That shows an inner strength not many woman have. Hell, if I saw what she saw, I don't think I would have been so understanding, or forgiving...but then again, I can be an asshole at times; just ask Blair and Keeton.

I've just hung up the phone after reconfirming our reservation at Lucio's and my mind flits to Stacey and her sexy ass. Picking up my phone, I quickly arrange a surprise for Stacey, and then I sit back in my chair and smile. Tonight, I'm going to knock her socks off. She will not be able to resist my charms. And that will start in the next ten minutes.

I'm going over this latest company's portfolio when my phone pings with a text. Picking it up. I don't recognize the number but I swipe to read it, it could be a new client, but it's not.

**UNKNOWN:** *Thank you for the lovely flowers.*
**Bennett:** *You are welcome. How did you get my number?*
**Stacey:** *I have my ways. \*\*wink\*\**
**Bennett:** *I bet you do. \*\*wink wink\*\**
**Bennett:** *See you in a few hours.*
**Stacey:** *Looking forward to it. \*\*winking face emoji\*\**

The rest of the afternoon flies by, and before I know it, I'm driving home to get ready for my date. Pulling up at my place, I sigh when I see a car parked out front. Not wanting to speak to her, I open my garage and pull in, bypassing her. Quickly, I press the button to close the garage door behind me, and thankfully, it closes before she has a chance to get to me.

Heading inside, I walk to the kitchen and grab a beer. Popping the cap on a Samuel Adams Sam '76, I bring the bottle to my lips and take a sip. Instantly, I relax as the sweet combination of lager and ale hits my taste buds, that is until there's a knock at my front door. "Bennett, I know you're home."

"No shit," I mumble to myself as I finish the rest of my beer. Taking a deep breath, I walk to the door and open it. "What?" I snap.

"That's no way to speak to the woman you love."

"Loved. Past tense. As is no more. What do you want?"

"I was hoping we—"

"Nope. Not interested, Amity. Now, if you excuse me, I have to be somewhere."

"I just want to talk," she whines, trying to step inside but I block her path. I know if she steps foot inside this house, she will never leave, and I don't ever want her in my space again. If I didn't love this house so much, I'd sell it and move, but she's already disturbed my life enough.

"No. Not tonight. I have somewhere to be."

She stares at me, an evil glint appearing in her eyes. "You can't ignore me forever, Benny."

"I hate when you call me Benny and forever will not be soon enough. Now, get the fuck off my property before I call the cops."

Stepping back, I slam the door in her face. Walking back to the kitchen, I uncap another beer and chug it back. Slamming the empty bottle on the countertop. "Fuuuuck!" I shout to the empty space. Shaking my head, I walk into my room to shower. Of course, she-devil would appear as soon as I take a chance with someone new, but I will not let her ruin this. She almost ruined me once but not this time.

---

Parking my G-class in front of Stacey's building, I find myself nervous as I exit my car and walk toward the front entrance. The doorman greets me, and after conferring with him, he allows me access and I head on up to collect Stacey for our date.

My palms become sweaty in the elevator on the way up, and I feel hot and anxious. However, as soon as the doors open on her level, all nerves dissipate and confident Bennett remains... that is, until she opens the door. Holy fucking sexy as all fuck.

"Stacey, you are breathtaking." She's wearing a simple midnight blue halter dress that accentuates every curve on her body. It shows just the right amount of cleavage, it leaves you wanting more. The material stops just above her knees and on her feet are a sexy as sin pair of black strappy heels that elongate her legs. Her dark locks have a slight wave and her makeup is simple. Elegant. Flawless. Stunning. But what I notice most is... her eyes. They are radiant and bright and I can't believe how much they look like my eyes; a beautiful hue of green that is currently shining back at me.

Blinking a few times, I realize she's speaking to me. "Sorry, what was that?"

"I said, you look pretty good yourself, Mr. Burnsteen." We stare at one another, the temperature in the hallway increasing as we continue to eye fuck one another. "Would you like to come in?" she offers.

Shaking my head, I lick my bottom lip. "Stacey, if I step through your door, I won't be able to control myself and we won't make it to dinner. I want tonight to be the first of many amazing nights together, so how about a rain check?"

She nods. "Sounds wonderful to me. Let me grab my handbag." She turns and I watch her intently as she steps away from me. I haven't seen her ass yet, but it's just as stunning in this dress as it was the other day at the office. She looks over her shoulder at me and winks, before stepping out of sight.

Reaching down, I adjust my cock, which is painfully pressing against my zipper. A few moments later, she has her coat and handbag. She steps into the hallway and locks the door behind her. She smiles at me. "Shall we?"

"We shall."

Offering her my elbow, she links her arm though and we head over to the elevator. The doors immediately open and we step in. She presses the button for the lobby and we each stare at the numbers above the door, subtly—not so subtly—checking each other out.

We arrive at the lobby and step out, she once again, loops her arm around my elbow. Stopping at the doors, I help her into her coat and then we exit her building. Ushering her to my car, I open the door but before she climbs in, I gently tug on her arm. She turns to face me and I lower my lips to hers for a quick kiss. And by a quick kiss, I mean we make out like teenagers beside my car for a few minutes. "And that's why I didn't go inside," I whisper against her lips.

She laughs and climbs in. Walking around the front of my car, I watch her closely and see she's just as nervously excited as I am. I cannot wait to see how the night plays out.

# CHAPTER 10

HOLY SHITBALLS, BATMAN, WHEN I OPENED MY DOOR AND SAW Bennett standing there in all his holy-fucking-hotness, I nearly died. This man is the epitome of sexy, and for some unknown reason, he wants to date me. Spend time with me. I'm nothing special but when I'm around him, he makes me feel like I'm the only person in the room. He makes me feel sexy and confident, no one has ever made me feel like this before.

That kiss before I hopped into his car was just as electric as our New Year's Eve kiss, and the one from the office other morning. We fit together perfectly, too perfectly, and I'm just waiting for it to all go to shit like it usually does for me.

My eyes are locked on him as he walks around the car to the driver's side, and I think that maybe I've never had luck with love because I start something with negative thoughts in my mind. Maybe it's time to start thinking positive, take Gage's advice that he gave Kasey, just go for it.

"Ready?" he asks, as he clips his seat belt in place.

Nodding my head, I respond, "Yep."

"Let's do this." He winks at me and then pulls away from the curb.

"Where are we going?"

"Lucio's, I hope you like Italian."

"I love Italian. I could eat pasta or pizza every day."

"Me too."

At the same time, we both ask, "Favorite topping?"

We both laugh, and then we both say, "Thin pepperoni."

Again, we both laugh. "Pepperoni on thin is seriously your fav?"

He nods, and glances toward me. "Seriously. No better topping. It's simple, but it's the best, but only on thin."

"Yes to that whole statement," I eagerly reply, my voice an octave higher with excitement.

"Add in ranch dressing and…"

I cut him off, "Ohh my God, yes!" I shout, and a little moan slips out as I think about it.

"You sound like you are about to climax."

"Pepperoni on thin with ranch dressing, wouldn't you?"

"Yeah, true, AND if it means I get to hear you make that sound again, I'll order it every time we are together."

The air around us electrifies and we were talking about pizza, this is going to be one hot, hot night.

We continue to chat and get to know one another. We are

sitting at a red light and I look to him. "I do have one question that's been niggling at me."

"Okay, shoot."

"The packages, what's in them?"

A laugh escapes his lips and he looks at me grinning. "Well, the first 'real' missed delivery was my limited edition Stephen King I'd just bought. The others were always the same empty box. I didn't trust the delivery punk to have anything of importance in it."

I laugh, "I like your style, Mr. Burnsteen."

"Why thank you, Ms. Thomms."

---

We arrive at the restaurant and Bennett parks the car. Ever the gentleman, he helps me out. Lacing his fingers with mine, we walk into Lucio's. He helps me with my coat and then we are met with the man himself, Lucio. "Bennett, how are you?"

"I'm good, Lucio. You?"

"Can't complain." Then his eyes land on me and he grins at Bennett. "And who is this exquisite beauty?"

"I'm Stacey," I say, offering my hand, but he grabs my upper arms and air kisses me.

He looks to Bennett. "Don't let this one go, Bennett, she's a keeper."

My cheeks tinge pink at his words, "Not planning on it," Bennett says and my cheeks darken further. Looking to him, he winks at me before Lucio takes my arm and ushers us to a table in the back. It's secluded and extremely romantic. Lucio pulls my chair out and I take a seat. "Thank you."

He nods and turns to Bennett, whispering something to him before he walks toward the kitchen.

Bennett takes a seat across from me. Our eyes lock. No words are spoken but the moment is perfect, absolutely perfect. A smile breaks free and I realize I'm happy, happier than I have been in a very long time.

Lucio returns with a bottle of red wine and an antipasto platter. The wooden board has a colorful arrangement of marinated vegetables, olives, rich cheeses, and cured meats. He places the board on the table and sets about opening the wine. "This wine is a Frontenac from Acquaviva Winery, just outside of Chicago here."

He opens the bottle and pours a little into my glass, offering me a taste. Lifting the glass, I swirl it around and breathe in, a slight moan escapes and when I bring my glass to my lips and drink, another one slips out. "MMMMM," I moan, Lucio beams at me.

"She really is a keeper," he says to Bennet, before he fills my glass and then fills up Bennett's. With a nod he says, "Godere." *Enjoy.* And he leaves the two of us alone with our appetizer and wine.

Bennett picks up his glass. "A toast."

"What shall we toast to?" I ask as I pick up my glass.

"To new beginnings," he offers.

"I like that. To new beginnings." We tap our glasses and each take a sip. Again I moan, "This is the most delicious wine I have ever had." Taking another sip, another moan slips free.

Bennett groans.

"Are you okay?" I question, worried that something is wrong and our date will be over before it's even begun.

"If you keep moaning like that, I will not be held accountable for what I do to you in the middle of this restaurant. My restraint is already at its limit."

My cheeks heat at his words. I can't help smiling and my clit throbs between my thighs. Normally, if someone said that to me, I'd shy away and rebuff them, but Bennett's words don't have that effect on me. They have the opposite effect, and I want to throw myself across the table at him and ravish him. The only thing stopping me is we are in a restaurant right now.

"Stacey, you are gorgeous and you don't even know it. You make everything you do look sexy."

"Says the gorgeous one," I counter.

We stare intently at one another, the air around us crackling with desire. My tongue darts out and I lick my bottom lip, his eyes drop and follow the movement. Suddenly, he stands up and walks around the table. Leaning down, he grips my cheeks and kisses me. His lips press against mine. My eyes droop closed but as quickly as he was there, he's gone again.

Blinking rapidly, I watch as he takes his seat back across from me. He takes a sip of wine and then pops an olive from the platter into his mouth. Once my breathing is back under control, and the air around us returns to normal, we fall into easy conversation and we have the most amazing night together.

Bennett and I click on so many levels. We are both from small families, whom we hold near and dear to us, but most of all, we are both passionate about wine, hiking, and 80s music. We both agree the 80s was the best decade for music, cheesy hair and dress sense aside.

Lucio brings out pepperoni on thin, with a side of ranch dressing, and the most amazing basil pesto pasta. The pasta looks like a pile of green snot, but oh my God, it's so tasty. I lose count at the amount of times I moan throughout the meal. And when the dessert platter is placed between us, I'm done for. There's tiramisu, Panna Cotta, semifreddo, cannoli, and three other decadent looking bite-sized items. I try them all, each one tastier than the last. We end the meal with a coffee, followed by a liqueur. Bennett has a Frangelico and I have a Limoncello.

By time we leave, I'm ready to explode, my tummy full. Wiping my mouth, I look to Bennett who is staring at me. "That was amazing, Bennett. Thank you for a lovely meal."

"My pleasure," he says with a wink.

We stand to leave and after Bennett settles the bill, Lucio walks us to the door. We say our goodbyes and promise to return soon. Bennett helps me into my coat and then we head to his car. The walk to the car is quick as the temperature has dropped rapidly while we were inside and snow has started to fall again.

Like before, he helps me into the car and he quickly rounds the hood. He starts the engine and looks to me. "Would you like to go to Acquaviva Winery with me tomorrow?"

Without pausing, I say, "I'd love to."

We drive back to my place in silence, but it's not uncomfortable. We pull up in front of my building, I invite him up but he declines, which surprises me. Hiding I'm upset about him not coming up, I lean over place a kiss on his cheek and climb out.

Dejectedly, I walk to the building entrance. Before I get to the doors, my arm is pulled. Bennet spins me around and slams his lips to mine. If I thought our kisses before were amazing, this one tops them all. He slides his hands into my hair and gently tugs. I gasp and he takes the opportunity to slip his tongue into my mouth. He dips me back and increases the pressure of our kiss. As quickly as he was kissing me, he pulls away and places me upright once again. Placing a kiss on the tip of my nose, he winks and walks back to his car. He climbs in and I'm still frozen on the spot. He lowers the passenger window. "Pick you up at 11:00 a.m.!" he shouts.

Words elude me so I nod my head in agreement. With a wave, he puts the window up and pulls away. Leaving me a quivering mess in front of my building. Shivering, I shake sense into myself and head inside. As I take the elevator up, I run my finger over my lips. They are still tingling from our goodbye kiss. I expected tonight to end between the sheets, so that was an unexpected ending to our night, but at the same time, it was perfect. I cannot wait for tomorrow and our second date.

# CHAPTER 11

Leaning back in my chair, I rub my belly and look to Bennett. "Oh my God, I'm so full. That food was amazing."

"It sure was," Bennett says, wiping his mouth with his napkin before placing it on his plate. He stares across the table, the heat in his eyes instantly warming me. "Would you like to take a walk through the vines before we drive back?"

"I'd like that."

We both stand from the table, he steps to me and places his hand on my lower back, ushering me out of the restaurant. Pulling our coats on, we step outside. The sun is shining. The sky is crystal clear, there's not a cloud in the sky, leading you into a false sense of warmth.

"It has warmed up a little," he says, pulling me closer to him. I fit under his arm perfectly, like I was made to snuggle with him.

With a laugh, I burrow closer into him. "I think it's the food and wine that did that, it's still fucking chilly, if you ask me."

"Well, I better warm you up then." He raises his eyebrows suggestively. Placing a kiss on my temple—swoon—we begin to walk down the path toward the vines. We come to a stop and stare at the view.

"Wow," I murmur, "It's gorgeous."

"Sure is," he huskily says, but when I look to him, I notice he's staring at me and not the view before us. My insides quiver at the intensity of his gaze. Internally I grin. On the outside, I shiver from the chill. "Come on, before you freeze to death on me." We continue to walk among the vines.

"But what a way to go," I say, "Gorgeous scenery. Full tummy. Amazing wine. Hot date. What better way to die?"

"You think I'm hot?" he asks.

"That's what you took from that?"

"Yep. And I concur, hottest date ever."

"Someone's high on themself."

"I wasn't referring to me."

We stop, I pull out from his side and face him, draping my arms over his shoulders I stare keenly at him. "Well, what specifically were you referring to?"

"You," he says. With that one word, I melt. I'm falling for this man hard and fast. Before I have time to think further on that, he grips my cheeks and presses his lips to mine. Closing my eyes, I give myself over to the kiss and him. Tightening my arms around his shoulders, I pull him closer to me. He walks us backward until my back hits a tree. He cocoons me in. I feel safe and warm in his embrace. He runs his palm down my body and slides his hand inside my jacket. Squeezing my ass, I moan into his mouth. He runs his thumb sensually along my jawline and down my throat as he slides his other hand between my thighs and cups my pussy, running his middle finger along my seam.

Instantly, my panties are soaked.

My hips begin to move and I grind myself on his palm and fingers. That tingly buzzing feeling begins to develop low in my belly, I'm going to come any minute. Just as I'm about to crash over the edge, he stop and removes his hand. My eyes pop open. Returning my stare, his gaze is just a heated as mine. Opening my mouth to speak, he removes his hand from my cheek and presses his finger to my lips. Then I realize that his other hand is popping open the button on my pants and lowering the zipper. Our eyes are locked on one another as he slides his hand inside my pants and underneath my panties. His finger brushes over my clit and I shudder. My orgasm, that was withheld only moments ago, begins to deliciously simmer again. Moving his finger between my lips, it slides with ease due to how wet I am. Bending his finger he pushes it inside me. He wriggles it around, hitting that magical spot over and over. Pulling out I whimper, but then he flicks my clit, sending shockwaves throughout my body. Sliding his hand down again, he pushes two fingers inside and begins to thrust them in and out. He is literally finger fucking me right now.

"Bennnnetttt," I moan.

My breathing is labored as he continues to pump his fingers in and out of me. I'm close to coming when he drops to his knees, pulls my pants and panties down to my knees. Leaning forward he sucks on my clit and presses his fingers back inside. The increased friction causes me to reach my climax and I explode. Gripping the sides of his head, I shove him farther into my core. Moaning in delight as he continues to suck and fuck me with his fingers.

Riding out my orgasm, I lean back into the tree and let the pleasure envelop me. My body relaxes and Bennett pulls away. Staring up at me, he grins. Even with my juices coating his chin, he is still the sexiest man I have ever seen.

Leaning down, I grip his cheeks and kiss him. He stands up but our lips remain connected. The moment is broken when we hear voices nearby. Quickly I pull my pants up my legs, but I don't have time fasten them before another couple joins us.

"It's beautiful here, isn't it?" the man says.

"It sure is," Bennett confirms, throwing a wink my way.

I'm nervous that they know what just happened, but as quickly as they appeared, they leave. Shaking my head, I quickly do up my pants. Bennett laughs. "Come on, I'll take you home," he says, lacing his fingers with mine.

Silently we walk to his car. The atmosphere now is awkward, and I wonder if what I just let him do to me has put me into the skanky ho category, and therefore, he now wants nothing to do with me.

My thoughts ramp up even more when we get back to my place, and just like last night, he kisses me goodbye and leaves.

What the hell?

# CHAPTER 12

As soon as I get into my apartment, I send an SOS text to the girls. I need to debrief, and no one will have better advice than my three best gals: Kasey, Marlee, and Chelle. Within the hour, they are all here. Wine is handed out, crackers and cheese is served. We take our usual spots in my living room; me on the floor by the fire but in reach of the coffee table, Marlee and Kasey on the love seat, each with their legs curled under them, and Chelle in my armchair. And when I say armchair, think of the throne type chair Victoria from *Revenge* sat in.

"Why won't he sleep with me? Am I that repulsive?" I whine

to Kasey, Marlee, and Chelle. The three of them shaking their heads side to side.

"Uh ah," Chelle says.

"No way in hell," Marlee offers.

"Don't be silly," Kase scoffs, giving me the eye. She then adds, "He went down on you at a winery and fingered you among the vines. No man would do that without wanting to seal the deal."

"But.."

She raises her hand and eyes me. "I bet, if it wasn't snowing and negative a billion, he would have fucked you right there,"

"Why don't you initiate it?" Marlee offers, "Dress sexy, march up to his office and ravage him."

My eyes pop wide open at her absurd sexy suggestion, and then I begin to nod my head in possible agreement. As I consider it, something else hits me. My eyes pop open even wider when I realize something from last week at the office. "Oh my God, is that what you and Gage did in his office last week?"

Marlee shrugs. "Hey, I'm pregnant and always horny."

"You're pregnant?" Kase and I squeal in unison.

"Ummm..." She looks to us, a guilty look on her face. "Surprise."

"Ohh my God," Kasey shouts and jumps toward Marlee, wrapping her arms around her. "That's so awesome. I'm so happy for you both."

We all share hugs and congratulations, then I pull the focus back to me. "Okay, Marlee, yay, you're knocked up, let's now focus on getting me laid so I can have what you three lucky hoes have."

They all laugh, but I'm serious. I want what they all have and for the rest of the afternoon, we concoct a plan for me to woo and get Bennett between the sheets. Once the plan is sorted, we have a fun-filled girly evening, which leads into a very drunken late night, well, drunken for everyone but Marlee.

It was just what I needed to calm my nerves and put everything in order for Monday afternoon.

---

First thing I did, when I arrived at work this morning, was call up to BKB and with the help of Barb, I have an appointment at 5:15 p.m. with Bennett, and he will not be able to resist me...I hope.

The day drags by at a snail's pace and finally, 5:00 p.m. rolls around and my workday is over. It's go time. Racing to the bathroom, I quickly change into my midnight blue wrap dress—easy to strip out of—and I tease my hair, giving it a bit of body. No need for a lingerie change because this morning, I made sure to wear sexy undergarments. Underneath my dress, I'm wearing a blush pink matching set. The bra makes my boobs look a-mahzing, and the high cut of the panties accentuates my legs...as do the killer, sky-high black pumps I'm wearing.

Touching up my lipstick, I give myself a once over and smile. "It's showtime," I say to the empty bathroom. Pressing the call button, a car arrives immediately and I step in.

When I step into reception, Barb grins at me and whistles. "Go on in. You'll be alone as I sent the other two bozos on a wild-goose chase for the afternoon."

"You rock, Barb. Thanks for this."

"It's my pleasure. I haven't seen Bennett this happy in a long time, and it's all because of you. I'll do anything to see that boy happy."

Smiling at her once more, I take a deep breath and walk down the hall toward his office. With each step I take, my heart rate accelerates, not with nerves or fear, but with excitement and joy…but it's short-lived when I push open the door to his office.

# CHAPTER 13
# BENNETT

Barb has been acting weird all day, actually everyone is in a weird mood today. Blair and Keeton disappeared around three, and it's just Barb and me in the office. My mind keeps flitting to Stacey, and each time I think about heading down to see her, I'm waylaid somehow. It's like the universe is conspiring to keep us apart.

It's nearing five when I decide I'll call it a day. Checking my calendar to see what I have tomorrow, I deflate when I see I have an appointment in fifteen minutes. I hate when Barb slips in last minutes meetings, and this one has no notes attached to it, so I have no idea what it's about. I'm frustrated now as I hate being unprepared.

I'm about to go out and see Barb to get more details, when the door to my office swings open and in waltzes Amity. *Fuck*, I internally yell.

"Amity," I snarl, standing up, I walk over to the bar in the corner and pour myself a drink. With my back to her, I throw it back and enjoy the burn of the single barrel malt as it slides down my throat. Happy that Barb restocked my favorite Jack Daniels variety. Pouring another, I turn to face my unwanted visitor—now I know why there was no appointment details— and I stare at the woman before me.

"Bennett, darling," she singsongs in her holier-than-thou voice, "we didn't get to finish our chat the other day."

"I was finished," I snap, I know I'm being an asshole right now, but this woman really grates on my nerves. Her cheating on me Chance Caplin, heir to the Caplin hotel chain, and ditching me twelve months ago was the best thing to ever have happened.

"Well, I wasn't. I was trying to tell you that things with Cappie have ended and I want you back."

"Did he comes to his senses and drop your sorry ass?"

"Benny, don't be like that."

"Stop fucking calling me Benny, my name is Bennett."

"Wow, rude much," she says as she sits down, her ridiculously short dress rising as she does. She notices me checking her legs out and she uncrosses them, giving me a look between her thighs. She smirks at me, "As I was saying, Cappie and I are no longer an item. I want us to get back together."

"Not gonna happen," I snarl.

"Benny, please," she whines. Standing up, she walks over to me and places her hand on my forearm. I shudder at her touch, especially when she starts to run her finger lazily up my arm and across to my chest.

Pulling back from her, she continues her fingers path to my chest. She leans in to kiss me. Gripping her upper arms I hold her at bay and shake my head, I'm about to tell her off when the door to my office swings open. Amity and I both turn our heads to see Stacey standing there, her mouth drops open in shock. She looks back and forth between Amity and me, and then her eyes land on my hands on Amity and from the look of utter devastation on her face, I know she's thinking the worst right now.

Amity smirks at Stacey and it causes my blood to boil.

Stacey shakes her head, turns on her heel, and races out before I can say anything. "Fuck," I growl. Pushing Amity to the side, I race after Stacey. "Stacey!" I yell down the corridor. I step into reception, just as the elevator doors are closing and my heart breaks at what I see. Stacey is crying and looks completely broken.

"Fuck." I groan, running my hands through my hair in frustration. Turning on my heel, I swing my arm out and swipe at the vase on the reception desk. It crashes to the floor, the glass shattering into a million pieces. Much like my heart right now.

Barb steps into reception and looks shocked. "Bennett, what happened?"

"Amity," I growl, and as if I summoned the she-devil herself; she steps into reception.

"Yes," she sweetly says.

"Get the fuck out of here, Amity. I N-E-V-E-R want to see you here again. If I do, I'll call security and have your ass thrown out. Do I make myself clear?"

"You cannot seriously be choosing her over me?"

"You bet your ass I am." Her mouth drops open in shock,

"Stacey is a million times the woman you are. If you just cost me her—"

"Bennett," Barb interrupts me. "Go after her. I'll clean this up," she looks to Amity, "And then I'll take out the trash."

"Thank you, Barb," I say.

Racing to the elevator, I repeatedly press the call button. "Come on. Come on." I chant, finally the doors open and I step in. The world clearly hates me right now because the elevator stops on every floor and then traffic is bedlam as I drive over to Stacey's.

Illegally parking out front, I race inside, wanting to see her and explain, but the concierge will not let me up. He calls her apartment but there is no answer. At the thought of losing her, I physically feel sick. This woman has captivated me and I hope like hell, it's not over before we even gotten a chance.

# CHAPTER 14

THE SIGNS WERE ALL THERE.

I'm such an idiot.

I should have trusted my instincts; he didn't sleep with me because he's sleeping with her, his fucking girlfriend.

"Asshole," I mumble to myself, garnering an unhappy look from the person next to me in the elevator. Muttering an apology, I lower my head, willing the tears to stay back. The doors open to WFOX-FM and I race to my desk.

Grabbing my things, I make a beeline for the stairs, but I don't get far before I hear Gage. "Stacey." His voice laced with concern. I don't want to talk to anyone right now, so I ignore him and keep walking. With the stairwell door in my line of sight, I push the door open, but before I can make my escape, he catches up to me and grabs my arm.

Spinning to face him, I sadly stare at him. Seeing the concern in his eyes opens the floodgates and I fall apart. He envelops me in a hug in the stairwell doorway and lets me cry. Once I have no more tears left to cry, he asks, "Stacey, you wanna talk about it?"

Shaking my head, I sniffle, "No."

"Do you want to come back to our place?"

Again, I shake my head. "No," I softly say, choking back a sob.

"Do you want a lift home?"

Nodding my head up and down. "Yes, please," I quietly murmur. He steps back into the office and on autopilot I follow him. I'm now thankful to have found Gage because the thought of hoping on the "L" home doesn't appeal to me right now. Nothing appeals to me right now...except maybe the death of Bennett and his bitch-faced whore.

"Just let me get my things and then we can go." He smiles at me, not sure how to act right now. He turns on his heel and races back to his office. Nodding again, I watch as he walks away, Marlee is right, he does have a fine ass. A little laugh breaks free, and then I think of Bennett and his mighty fine ass and that crushing pain hits me square in the chest with the force of a 747 taking off. The elevator ding causes my eyes to widen and fear to take hold. *He's here* is my immediate thought. Holding my breath, I watch the doors open and sigh in relief when I see that it's just the cleaning crew.

Gage reappears and he guides me toward the elevator. He presses the button and when the doors open, I'm glad but also upset to see it's empty. *Of course it's empty, he's up in his office having sex with that whore, like you had planned to do.* At that thought, I lift my hand to my mouth and swallow back another sob. Gage places his arm around my shoulder. The comfort feels nice, but at the same time it reminds me of being with asshat, and the tears I was holding back break free. We walk through the parking garage to Gage's car and I continue to cry.

He helps me into my seat, again sadly smiling at me as he closes my door. Buckling my belt, I rest my head against the window and let the grief overtake me. Sobbing like a baby, Gage drives me home. He doesn't say anything, he knows that right now I need silence…and a huge bottle of wine.

We pull up at my place and my door immediately swings open. My heart stops and I think it's him, but it's not. "Ohh, Stace," Kasey says, as she leans into the car and wraps her arms around me. She's the exact person I need right now. Then over her shoulder, I see both Marlee and Chelle standing on the sidewalk. Seeing them here causes the floodgates to open again, and I completely fall apart.

My three best friends assist me inside. And by assist, I mean two of them drape their arms around me and usher me to the building, while the third takes the flank and opens doors and leads the way. Once inside, wine is poured and they let me blurt it all out. It takes a while since I'm a snotty, teary mess. "I guess it's better this happened now than after I fell in love with the asshole."

They ply me with enough wine to sink a ship and I pass out on my couch. Still dressed in my killer dress and sexy underwear. When I wake the next day, I feel like shit. *That happens when you drink*, looking to the coffee table I count four bottles, *a crap ton of wine with your girls*. And in the light of the new day, I don't feel any better.

Picking up my phone to check the time, I see a text from *him*. I don't need to slide it open to see what it says, four words stare back at me. Four words that will no doubt be followed by a lie.

**Bennett:** *We need to talk.*

Unlocking my phone, I delete the message and then notice he's left me a voicemail as well. Not wanting to listen to his lies, I delete it without listening to it. Standing up, I walk into my bathroom and take a shower. Turning the water hotter than I usually would, I step under the flow. Closing my eyes, I let the droplets wash over me. I feel like I could cry again but I don't think I have any more tears left in me. After a few moments, I take a deep cleansing breath and begin to wash myself. Stepping out, I dry off and in a robotic manner; I go about getting ready for work.

I've just slipped on my shoes when there's a knock at my door. I freeze. What if it's him? I don't want to face him ever again. The decision is made for me when I hear Marlee. "Babe, it's me, open up."

Walking over to the door, I swing it open to be met with her and Gage. Coffee in hand. "You are a life saver," I say, as I take the coffee from her. Taking a sip, I sigh as the caffeine goodness hits my taste buds.

"How you feeling?" Marlee asks, as she and Gage enter my apartment.

"Considering how much wine I drank last night, pretty good." She gives me the stare that says, 'Not what I'm talking about.' Sighing, I bite my lip, "Ummm, not sure to be honest. He, umm, ahh, texted me."

"What did it say?" she asks, as she picks up the bottles of wine from the coffee table and places them in the recycling. I notice Gage is in the kitchen stacking the dishwasher for me.

Sadly I smile, I may have shitty taste in men, but I have great taste in friends.

"Stace," she shouts, gaining my attention again, "What did it say?"

"'We need to talk.' I deleted it without replying. There was also a voice mail but I did the same thing."

"Don't you think you should hear him out?" Gage says, garnering an evil look from Marlee, who's sitting on the sofa in her usual spot.

"No," she scoffs, "The ass does not—"

"Just hear me out," he interrupts, as he takes a seat on the lounge next to his fiancée. "Things aren't always what they seem—"

Now it's my turn to interrupt, "No, there was no misinterpreting. She had her hands on him. She was smiling, he looked shocked. You don't look shocked when there's no guilt to be had."

"I just think you need to talk to him," Gage says.

"Gage," Marlee growls. "Go start the car, we'll be down in a sec."

The two of them have a silent conversation. He stands up, kisses her temple, and leaves, with no argument. This is a side of Gage I'm not used to seeing, Marlee has him wrapped around her pinky finger. I smile, it's nice to see our resident Grinch happy…I wonder if I'll get my happily ever after like him?

Plopping onto the coffee table, in front of her, I look over at her. "Should I hear him out?"

"Do you want to hear him out?" She throws my question back at me, making me think; *do* I want to hear him out?

I shrug. "I don't know what I want."

"Can you handle the truth?" she asks me, and a laugh escapes me as I picture Jack Nicolson and Tom Cruise. In my mind, I yell, *You can't handle the truth*, and I think that might be true. *Can* I handle it if what I saw was true? Shaking my head, I realize Marlee is still talking to me. "....what if what you saw wasn't as it appeared? What if you let him get away due to a misunderstanding? Will you be able to handle that you walked away from something which could have been amazing?"

"I don't know, but if I'm honest, the unknown and uncertainty is killing me."

"Then there's your answer," she matter-of-factly says.

Nodding my head, I agree, but I'm scared because what if I don't like what I hear?

# CHAPTER 15

Catching a lift into work with Marlee and Gage, we drop Marlee at Chicago Hopes for Kids and then Gage and I head to the office. I'm a nervous Nellie as we hop into the elevator up to WFOX-FM. A part of me hopes he's there, but a part of me also never wants to see his sexy face again. Then there's the side that's so confused; she doesn't know what she wants when it comes to Bennett Burnsteen.

We step into reception. It's empty and I deflate, I guess I *did* want him to be here. But sitting on my desk is the most amazing bunch of tulips in a tall glass vase. "I think that there," he points to the vase, "says everything," Gage says to me.

Scrunching my eyes in confusion, I ask, "Huh?"

"If he was with that other woman, he wouldn't be sending you flowers." He pauses and then adds, "and if he does, he's a fucking dog and you are better off without him."

"How do you know they are from him?" I question, but as the words leave my mouth, I know they are. I don't know why I feel I know this, but I just do.

"There's only one way to find out," he says, and he watches me as I walk toward my desk. Stopping beside it, I take a deep breath and pick up the envelope resting against the vase. Pulling the card out, my eyes water with tears as I read.

STACEY,
FLOWERS ARE NOT ENOUGH TO SAY HOW SORRY I AM.
THERE IS *NOTHING* BETWEEN AMITY AND ME. SHE'S A
THORN IN MY SIDE THAT WILL NOT GO AWAY. IF YOU'LL
ALLOW ME, I'D LOVE TO HAVE DINNER WITH YOU
TONIGHT. I WANT THIS BETWEEN US. YOU ARE THE
LIGHT I NEED IN MY LIFE.
STACEY, YOU ARE EVERYTHING I DIDN'T REALIZE I
WANTED.
YOURS, IF YOU'LL HAVE ME,
B xo

Looking over to Gage, he smiles. "Go, I'll man reception."

Pushing away from my desk, I race to the stairwell and I haul ass up one floor. I'm huffing and puffing when I get there. Taking a few moments, I calm my breathing and then push the door open. I use a little too much force and it crashes against the wall with a bang.

Two people turn toward me and I instantly deflate. Standing at the reception desk with Barb is Amity.

"Please leave," Barb snarls. I guess that's my answer. Turning to the stairwell door, I feel a hand on my shoulder. "Not you," she softy says, as she shakes her head. She turns to face Amity and growls, "Her." She emphasis the word *her* and points to the woman. "Amity, you are no longer welcome at BKB Incorporated."

"You can't do that," she snaps.

"Yes, she can," Bennett booms from the other side of the room. "Amity, I made myself clear yesterday."

"But, Benny—"

"NO!" he shouts. "Amity, YOU need to leave. Now. I never want you to come back. We are done. We have been done since you cheated on me. Actually, we were done before then, but I was too stupid to see it." His eyes land on mine. "Besides, I've met someone else." He stares intently at me and smiles, a smile that shoots straight to my heart. "She is more woman than you will ever be. She's everything you are not. She's perfect in every way that matters. She's sexy. Feisty. Fun. Carefree and enigmatic. She's means everything to me, and I hope I'm everything to her."

"You're choosing her," she point at me, "over me?" Pointing back to herself, her voice laced with shock. Her face etched with confusion.

"Yep," he states. That one word means the world to me.

Bennett strides past her, over to me. Before I have a chance to say anything, he grips my cheeks and presses his lips to mine. The spark that was there before jolts between us stronger than ever when our lips meet. The air becomes electrified as we kiss. *This is the best kiss of my life.* Everything around me disappears, angels sing. Doves fly. Fireworks explode. The only thing I notice is Bennett's lips on mine and his hands searing my cheeks. Our kiss deepens. His tongue sweeps against mine. His lips firmly press to my lips.

Breaking the connection, he pulls backs and gazes into my eyes. "Hi."

"Hi." I manage to stutter as I stare at the man before me.

Movement from behind him has my eyes popping wide open, security is here and they are escorting Amity toward the elevator. "Benny, please," she begs.

"Thanks, guys," Bennett says, ignoring her pleas and cries as she is escorted into the waiting elevator.

Lacing his fingers with mine, he pulls me across reception, down the corridor, and into his office. He spins around to face me, as he pushes the door closed and steps toward me. Stepping back, my back hits the wooden door and he cocoons me in. We stare intently at one another. The hazel of his eyes is electric and focused solely on me. The golden hue bores into me. My breathing is rapid, "Stacey—"

Pressing my finger to his lips, I stop him. "I know. I'm sorry I overreacted. I've…" my eyes drop to the floor, this is deeper than I intended, and I'm not sure I can articulate what I want to say.

He places his finger under my chin and lifts so I'm staring at him again. "You've what?"

"I've never felt like this before about someone."

"Me either," he agrees. "Stacey, you have knocked me off my perch. Instead of falling into a million pieces, I've taken flight, and when you are around, I feel like I can conquer anything thrown at me."

"Me too," I quietly whisper.

"The look on your face yesterday cut me deep."

"What I saw shattered me."

"I'm so sorry. Amity is in my past." He places emphasis on that word. "There is nothing left between us. Please believe me."

"I do, I do believe you. Now shut up and kiss me."

"With pleasure."

He lowers his head to mine and covers my mouth with his. This kiss is soft yet hard. Frantic yet calm. It's full of passion and desire. He lowers his hands to my ass and lifts me up. Wrapping my legs around his waist, I feel his erection between us. I smile into the kiss when I realize what I came for yesterday is about to happen. He walks over to the sofa and lowers me down. He settles himself on top of me and somehow manages not to squish me.

Unashamedly, I grind myself against him. We both moan into the kiss. My panties are completely soaked. His cock is rock-hard pressing into me. Reaching down between us, I pop open the button on his pants and lower his fly; he sighs in relief at the additional space. Sliding my hands around to his ass, I squeeze before pushing the material down. He lifts up and shimmies them off, kicking them to the side. While he's lifted up, I slide my pants and panties down to my knees.

He lowers down and kisses me frantically again. "This isn't how I expected our first time," he says against my lips.

"It was what I was here for yesterday," I reply back.

"Then it's perfect," he declares, as he slides his cock up and down my core.

With our eyes locked on one another, he inches the tip inside. A moan slips from my lips and I raise my hips to assist him. Ever so slowly, he sides all the way in. My walls clench and hug his cock. Pulling out, he slides back in quickly, repeating the process over and over. Wrapping my arms around his neck, I pull him down for a kiss. He rocks his hips and continues to thrust in and out. Our tongues slip in and out of each other's mouth in sync to what's happening below.

Out of nowhere, my orgasm detonates and I shatter beneath

him. My body quivering as pleasure courses through my body. His thrusting halts and he grunts out his own orgasm. His body trembling above me as he releases his seed within me.

My eyes pop open when I realize we didn't use protection, and from the look on his face he's just realized too.

"I'm so sorry, Stacey,"

Shaking my head, I cup his face in my palm. "It's fine, it takes two to tango, it's fine." I realize I said it's fine twice but really, I'm not freaking out.

The moment is interrupted when the door to his office opens, "OUT!" Bennett bellows as he lifts his head toward the door.

"Ohh fuck, look at your lily white ass," Blair says with a laugh. He pauses. "Hey, Stacey."

"Get out, asshole," Bennett screams again.

Lifting my hands to my face, I begin to laugh. "Oh my God," I giggle into my hands, "This is why I booked an afterhours appointment yesterday."

Bennett stares down at me and before long, he too is laughing. With his softening cock still inside of me, we laugh and laugh at what's just occurred. Blair must have closed the door while we were laughing because Bennett looks up and he smiles. "Coast is clear," he says as he stands up. "I have a private bath over there." He points to a door on the opposite wall.

"Thanks." I shyly say, as I bend down and pull up my pants. I quickly walk over to the bathroom and close the door behind me. Leaning against the wood, I sigh and shake my head. That isn't what I expected to happen this morning.

Walking over to the toilet, I sit down and shake my head. I can't believe what just happened, not the Blair interruption but the sex with Bennett. It was out of the world amazing and totally worth the wait…but next time, we need to use protection.

# CHAPTER 16
# BENNETT

HOLY FUCKING SHIT, I JUST HAD OUT OF THIS WORLD SEX WITH Stacey. Unprotected, out of this world sex...in my office, but wow, it was fucking hot. After the disaster that was yesterday and Amity, I did not think I'd get my chance back with her, but I guess fate had other plans—*Thank you for not being a bitch today*.

If Blair hadn't barged in, I would have totally fucked her again. After one time, I'm addicted to this woman, and I will do everything in my power to keep her.

She steps back into my office and her eyes zero in on my package. It's then I realize, I'm standing in my office, with my cock out, and pants on the floor. "Shit," I mumble. Bending down, I quickly pull them up. Looking to Stacey, I see she's grinning at me. "Can I help you?"

She shakes her head. "Nope. I'm good."

We stare at one another. It's heated and if someone wasn't knocking on my door right now, I'd be bending her over the end of my desk and slamming my cock into her from behind. Walking to the door, I open it to see Blair standing there with his eyes covered. "Is it safe?" he cheekily says.

"Yes," I snarl.

"Thank God, don't want to see your albino ass again." Looking to Stacey he teasingly adds, "Wouldn't mind seeing yours, though." He winks at her before walking over to my couch. Her eyes bug out at his response, but it doesn't surprise me. I shake my head and shrug toward Stacey. He goes to sit on the sofa but at the last minute, decides to sit in the armchair. Leaning back, he rests his left leg on his right thigh and his elbow on the arm. "Sooo, how's it going?"

"Fine, thanks for asking," Stacey says, as if the encounter not ten minutes ago didn't occur. She steps over to me. "I have to get to work."

Nodding my head, I lick my bottom lip. "Okay. Can I see you later?"

She nods and smiles. "I'd like that. Due to my unexpected detour this morning, I'll need to stay late, but if I work through lunch, I should be done by sixish."

"I'll come down and pick you up at six."

"I'd like that." She rests her palms on my cheek and places a featherlight kiss on my lips. Stepping around me, she exits my office. Poking her head back in, she looks to Blair. "Bye, Blair."

"Laters, Babycakes."

She laughs at his reply and walks away. Leaving me with a

smirking, grinning Blair. "Did you need something?" I ask, as I take a seat on the sofa.

"You going to clean that?" he asks.

"Clean what?"

"That sofa. It's got sex germs now."

"I quite like the sex germs," I say, leaning back, I rest my arm along the top. "Did you actually need something? Or were you just here to bust my balls?"

"Was coming to see if you were okay, Barb filled Keet and me in on what happened with she-devil yesterday afternoon and this morning."

"Yeah, I'm fine. The last twelve hours have been rough." I explain from my point of view, what happened yesterday afternoon and his eyes go wide. "Barb has also advised security not to let her into the building. Her visitation rights have officially been revoked."

"You should have done that long ago." Nodding my head, I agree with him. "How did you manage to sweet talk Stacey?"

"I have no idea. I sent her flowers and I apologized sincerely. Then in front of she-devil, I let everything I was feeling for her flow out and I kissed her passionately in front of Amity." His eyes pop open in shock and then he grins. "I threw everything I had into the kiss and then, well, you can guess what happened after."

"Must have been some kiss," Blair says, shaking his head in amusement and possibly shock; he knows I'm not one for PDAs.

"It was the best kiss ever."

"You have become a love sick fool." He pauses. "It's about time you moved on from bitch face." He laughs, "I wish I could have been there to see the look on her face when she realized you weren't going to choose her."

"I wish I could have seen it too."

Scrunching his face up in confusion and squinting, he says. "But you were there."

"BUT my eyes were focused on Stacey." Looking to Blair, I lean forward and rest my elbows on my knees, "Dude, I have never felt like this about a woman before. She has completely captivated me. Call me a pussy, whatever, I don't care. I'm falling for Stacey Thomms."

"The teasing will come later, but for now, I'll just say, I'm happy for you."

"Thanks, man."

Leaning over, we bump knuckles. I'm surprised at Blair's maturity about this, until he opens his mouth next, that is. "Now, when you find your balls, come meet Keet and me in the conference room, we need to discuss tactics for the Straya Inc. project."

"And there is it." He shrugs, "Give me five and I'll be there."

"You'll need more than five minutes to find those balls of yours. They are goneski, but I do kinda like the woman who has them firmly in her grasp."

"Get the fuck out of my office before I remove yours."

Blair stands up and squeezes my shoulder as he walks behind the sofa. I watch him exit my office. The door closes behind him and I realize that for once, he's right. Stacey does own my balls, per se, and I couldn't be happier for her to have them.

# CHAPTER 17

THE DAY FLIES BY AND BEFORE I KNOW IT, BENNETT IS EXITING THE elevator and walking toward me. Smiling at him as he walks across reception, I take the opportunity to check him out. He really knows how to rock a suit. "Hey there," he says, his voice so rough and deep, it vibrates through my body from head to toe.

"Hey yourself," I say, as I stand up and lean over my desk for a kiss. He places his lips against mine but he quickly pulls back. He stares into my eyes and he can see a flicker of sadness reflecting in mine. "Stace, babe, if I kissed you longer, I wouldn't be held accountable for what would happen to you right here on your desk. It's safer for your job that I pulled back."

"Then let's get out of here."

"Sounds good to me."

Turning on the answering machine, I grab my handbag and step around my desk. Bennett laces his fingers with mine and we make our way to the elevator. It arrives immediately and we both step in. Pressing the button for the parking garage, we begin our descent. The air in the elevator car is heated and crackling. The doors open and we step out and toward his SUV. "This is a pretty slick car," I tell him.

"Yeah, it is, right?"

"What made you choose this sexy beast of a car?"

"You remember the show *Revenge*?" I nod my head and think of my Bitchtoria throne chair, "Nolan drove one. I thought it was badass and when I made seven figures, I decided to treat myself."

"We all need to treat ourselves from time to time. When I landed my full-time gig at WFOX-FM, I bought myself this," lifting my purse, "it's a Balenciaga. I did eat ramen noodles for a whole month to be able to afford it, but what's one month when I have this gorgeous handbag."

When I look back at Bennett, I notice he's staring intently at me. "What?"

"You deserve the best in life, Stacey. You are exquisite."

My cheeks darken with embarrassment at his compliment. "Thank you. You deserve everything too. AND you are also exquisite, in more ways than one."

"Really, how so?" he questions, as he opens my door for me.

"You just are," I say. Before I climb in, I rest my palms on his chest and press my lips to his. He wraps his arms around my shoulders, pulling me close to him. Sliding mine around his sides, I run them up and down his back, paying close attention to his ass. Against his lips, I pant, "I don't think I can wait to get back to your place."

Without saying a word, he pulls me away from the car. Our lips still connected in a fierce and heated kiss. He slams the passenger door closed behind me and opens the back door. Effortlessly, he lifts me up onto the back seat. I shimmy back and he climbs in, pulling the door closed behind him. He hovers above me, with our eyes connected. I reach down and undo my pants, lower the zipper and pull them, and my panties, down my legs. Using my feet, I kick them off completely and spread myself open to him.

"You have the sexiest pussy," he says, as he slides a finger between my lips. Dipping it inside, he removes it and spreads my wetness all around. Gliding his digit over my clit, I moan. Lifting my hands, I lift up my blouse and squeeze my breasts over my bra. My nipples pucker beneath the satin, pulling the cup down, I pinch the tip between my thumb and forefinger. I moan and let the pleasure envelop me.

His eyes flick from between my legs to my hands at my chest. "Fuck me," he growls.

"Yes, please," I moan.

With a grin, he frees his cock, sheathes it with a condom he pulls from his pants pocket, and lines it up at my entrance. With his eyes locked on mine, he slides in. We both moan as my pussy clenches around him. He thrust his hips back and forth. Leaning down, he takes a nipple into his mouth and gently sucks.

"Bennett," I moan.

"Harder," I pant.

"Faster," I mewl.

"Yes!" I scream.

"BBBBB-eeeennnnn-eeeee-ttttt," I stutter.

He slides his hand between us and presses my clit, that's the detonation I need. I explode, screaming incoherent babbling into his mouth as I soar through my climax. My body is still trembling when he pulls back and I feel his body shudder above me, as he too reaches his climax.

We are both panting, sweaty, and completely sated. "Wow," I say, "That was…"

"Yep."

He lowers himself down and presses his lips to mine. We make out like teenagers at the drive-in on a Saturday night. We are both lost in the moment, it isn't until we hear the engine of a nearby car that we pull apart. Looking behind me, I realize that the windows are all fogged up. A giggle breaks free. "Oh my God, Bennett, we just had sex in the parking garage at work. What's wrong with us?"

He shrugs his shoulders and begins to laugh. "Your face right now is priceless."

"Shut up," I say, as I smack him in the chest. "Put that," I point to his cock, "away and let's get out of here before anyone we know sees us."

Without saying a word, he removes the condom, dropping it into his pants pocket, he puts his cock away, and zips his pants back up. Once he's semi-dressed, he helps me shimmy my pants back into place. He *helps* by squeezing my boob, before lifting my bra back into position. He gives my boob one more squeeze before lowering my shirt. Now that we are both dressed again, he opens the door and climbs out. He offers me his hands and I place mine in his and step out. When I look up, I see Gage walking toward us. My heart rate increases and my cheeks darken. When he sees us, he looks on in confusion. "Stacey, I thought you left a while ago?"

"I...umm...ahh," I'm a bundle of nerves right now, "went to see Bennett but he was busy—"

"Fucking you in my car," Bennett murmurs, but it's not as quiet as he thinks and Gage's eyes bug out of his head.

"Ohhhhhhh, I cannot wait to tell Marlee this," he teases.

"You are an asshole," I scoff.

"Me or him?" Bennett asks.

"Both of you." Looking to Bennett, I shake my head. "Can we go please?"

"Try actually starting the car this time," Gage teases. "Have a great night." He winks at us before he walks over to his car.

We stand and watch him walk away. "The girls are totally going to have a field day with this," I mumble to myself, shaking my head.

"Who cares?" Bennett says as he opens my door, "Did you have fun?" Nodding my head, my lips lift in a smirk. "Then who cares. Everybody fucks, most people just do it in a bed."

"Or in a car...or an office...Oh my God, I just realized that both times we have been caught by someone. From now on, bedroom sex only."

"What if I wanted to fuck you against the front door? Or in my kitchen? Or on the patio? Or go down on you in the shower?"

"There are always exceptions to the rules."

"I like your way of thinking, Ms. Thomms."

"Thank you, Mr. Burnsteen, now take me home and we can try sex in a bed."

"Again, I like your way of thinking."

And Bennett lives up to his expectations. That evening we

have sex in his bed, and then in a few other rooms of his house too. And each time is just as amazing as the last. We will definitely need to stock up on condoms. I'm falling hard and fast for this man, and I've never felt happiness like the before in my life. I don't ever want to stop feeling like this.

# CHAPTER 18

...February 14th, 2020

FOR THE FIRST TIME IN YEARS, I HAVE A DATE ON V-DAY. A DATE with a real man and that man so happens to be someone I've fallen head over heels for. When I think about it, it's the first time in years that I have a boyfriend on this day. Normally I hide at home, eat pizza, and watch Netflix. Not this year, this year, Bennett has invited me over to his place for a romantic dinner for two.

The last few weeks with him have been amazing. After the

Amity drama at the beginning, he and I fell into our relationship with ease. And the sex, Oh my God, it's off the charts amazing. It's never been this amazing before and the number of times we've done things in public, I've lost count. He brings out my inner minx.

Slipping on a black halter dress that hugs my curves and accentuates the girls, I straighten my hair and apply some lipstick. Sitting on the edge of my bed, I put on my strappy wedge heels and I'm ready to go. Pulling on my coat, I grab my handbag and head over to Bennet's for our V-Day dinner. I'm about to lock my door, when I remember the presents. Racing back inside, I pick them up off the hall table and head out, this time with everything that I need.

Buying his gift was hard. We haven't been dating for long, but I wanted to get him something special without it being corny or tacky. Kasey and I walked around the mall for what felt like days when I spotted a gift that will be perfect for us both. Tugging on her arm, I pointed to the store window display and she nodded her head immediately. Walking into the store, I grabbed the 'Sexy Truth-or-Dare' game. As I was walking to the register, I spotted a sexy sheer black teddy with red lips all over, with a matching G-string for me, and for Bennett, matching boxer briefs in the same print. It's fun. It's sexy. It's totally us, so I grab that too.

Pulling up to Bennett's house I smile. It's not the type of house I expected him to live in, but at the same time, after getting to know him, it suits him perfectly. It's a Cape Cod style that kind of reminds me of a gingerbread house. Walking up the stairs to his front porch, I become nervous but the door swings open and when my eyes land on Bennett—all nerves disappear —replaced by arousal and hunger. He's wearing jeans and a charcoal gray Henley that stretches across his chest, accentuating his muscles. My eyes roam over him and eventually land on his face, his smiling face, and I notice that he too is checking me out.

"Stacey, you look stunning." He leans forward and places a kiss on my cheek, just skimming my lips. My skin tingles when he pulls back. We stare at one another, the air around us warming, even with the chill from outside at my back. Our heads move toward one another, but the moment is broken when I car revs its engine, tires squealing as it takes off and flies down the street. We both turn our heads but all we see is smoke in the air.

"Damn hoods," Bennett says.

With the moment broken, he steps aside to let me in. The door closes behind me and my senses are enveloped in a tantalizing aroma. "Wow, dinner smells amazing," I say, as he helps me out of my coat and hangs it in the hall closet.

"It's lasagna," he says, as he turns to face me after closing the coat closet. "I hope you like it."

"You know I love lasagna and I'm sure I'll love yours too."

"I'm sure you will." He has a mischievous look in his eye as he says this, but before I can probe him, he slides his arm around my waist, pulls me to him, and presses his lips to mine. Against my lips me whispers, "Happy Valentine's Day, Stace."

"Happy Valentine's Day to you too," I reply, before pressing my lips harder to his. My tongue sweeping into his mouth, exploring hungrily, my insides quivering with anticipation of what's to come.

Breaking the kiss, he takes my hand in his and pulls me into his house. Stepping into the open plan room, my mouth drops open. There's millions, well it feels like millions, of tea light candles scattered around the room. The fire is crackling away, adding to the ambiance of the candles. The table is set for two, and off to the side is a gorgeous bunch of flowers, the same style as what he sent to me a few weeks ago.

"Bennett," I say as I turn to him. "This is gorgeous."

"Not as gorgeous as you." He wraps his arms around my waist, pulling me into his chest. He nuzzles my neck. Closing my eyes, I lean my head back, giving him access to my throat. His tongue licks up my neck, turning my head to face him, he kisses me. Like before, our tongues explore each other's mouth. Running, my hands up the back of his neck, I pull him into me. Increasing the pressure of the kiss. Gently tugging on his hair, I whisper, "I have a gift for you."

Lifting the gift bag, I turn to face him. "I thought we said no gifts."

Nonchalantly, I shrug my shoulders and hold out the gift bag to him. He takes it from me and lifts my hands to his lips, placing a kiss on my knuckles. He places the gift bag on the kitchen counter and pulls out the first present, he lifts the lid on the box and grins at me, "Sexy Truth-or-Dare, we will definitely play this later."

Nodding with a grin, I nudge my head to the bag. "There's one more in there."

He pulls out the tissue paper wrapped outfits, he tears into it and the teddy falls to the floor. Bending down, he picks it up and holds it by the straps, "Ummm, I think this will look better on you than on me."

"Der," I playfully laugh. "That's for me," I pick up the briefs, "these are for you."

"No way in hell am I wearing them," he snaps, grabbing the briefs from my hands.

"Ohh come on, please?" I whine and give him puppy dog eyes.

"Nope," he sternly says, dropping the briefs back into the gift bag.

"Then I won't be wearing this." I reach for the teddy and drop it into the bag on top of his discarded briefs.

"You don't play fair."

"If it sweetens the deal, I'll forgo the G and just wear the teddy?"

He swallows deeply. "You drive a hard bargain, Ms. Thomms."

Stepping to him, I grab his cock through his pants, "I promise to make you harder than ever before." Kissing his jaw, I gently nip him. Pulling back, I look up at him. "Do we have a deal, Mr. Burnsteen?"

"Yes," he moans, as I continue to squeeze his cock.

"Good answer." Pressing my lips to his, I wrap my arms around his neck and rub myself on his cock. He grips my ass, pulling me to him, my chest pressing into his. Our kiss is hungry and carnal. I'm ready to tear his clothes off and have my way with him when the oven timer beeps, interrupting our moment.

"Dinner's ready," he says into my mouth.

"We can reheat it," I murmur back, as I press myself farther into him.

He pulls back and we stare at one another. Chests heaving. Our eyes full of hunger for each other, not for food. My stomach growls, loudly. "Looks like someone hungry."

Nodding my head, I bite my lip. "Yeah…but not for food."

"For what I have in store later tonight, you are going to need *all* your energy. Especially since you have outfits for us to try out."

My eyes pop wide open at his statement. "Fine," I relent. "Feed me then."

"I promise to make it worthwhile."

"You better," I pout. He kisses my cheek and steps around me, heading to the kitchen.

"Can I help with anything?"

He stops and shakes his head side to side. "Nope, I've got it. You sit down and relax."

He steps back to me, and gently kisses the tip of my nose before turning and walking into the kitchen. I take the opportunity to check out his ass, *such a nice ass*. I take a seat at the table and watch him flit about the kitchen. *A girl could get used to this.* He returns with two plates, each with an individual lasagna and a side salad. He places them on the table, one in front of me and one for him. He races back to the kitchen and returns with garlic bread and a bottle of red.

Leaning forward, I close my eyes and breathe in the aroma: cheese, tomato, and garlic permeate the air and again my stomach grumbles. We both laugh as Bennett takes his seat. He pours us each a glass and raises his. "To us, on Valentine's Day. May we have many more together."

"I'll drink to that."

We gently tap our glasses and each take a sip. The wine is smooth and slides easily across my palette. Licking my lips, I look to Bennett and find him staring at me. "What?"

"You are exquisite, Stacey Thomms. I'm so glad that little shit delivered my package to you and was such an ass. These last few weeks with you have been the best. After our New Year's Eve kiss, I knew 2020 was going to be amazing."

A smile breaks free on my face. "I agree, I cannot remember ever being this happy."

We gaze at one another across the table, the only sound in the room is the crackle from the fire. Leaning over, I place a kiss on his lips. "I love you," I whisper against his lips.

"I love you, too," he whispers back.

Sitting back down, I pick up my knife and fork and cut into the lasagna. Forking a bite, I bring it to my mouth and moan when the flavors hit my taste buds. Through my mouthful, I mumble, "Oh my God, Bennett, this is amazing. It tastes just as good as the one at Lucio's."

He smiles. "Glad you think so."

He cuts into his and we chat about our day. A few mouthfuls later, his eyes bug out. "What's wrong?"

He shakes his head. "Nothing. Do you want dessert now?" he hastily asks.

"No, I'm still enjoying this," I say, as I cut into the lasagna again.

"Make sure there's room."

"Okay," I say, as I continue to eat. Glancing at Bennett, he looks worried. "Are you sure you're okay?"

He nods his head and takes a big gulp of wine.

"Are you worried that I'm going to figure out this lasagna is from Lucio's and you didn't cook it?"

His eye pop open and he sheepishly asks, "How did you know?"

"Well, the serving ramekin is very similar to the one from Lucio's. I was suspicious when I tasted it, and it was on par with his, but the deal breaker was when I discovered his restaurant name on the bottom after my second mouthful."

"Shit," he scoffs. "I'm sorry I kinda sorta lied."

"Kinda sorta?"

"Okay, I'm sorry I tried to pass of Lucio's lasagna as my own."

"I'm not, I got to eat lasagna from Lucio's and tease you about it. It's win/win for me." Raising my eyebrows I grin and take another sip of wine. "But most of all," I lower my voice and reach across the table to squeeze his hand, "I get to spend the evening with you."

We never got around to playing Sexy Truth or Dare, or wear our matching outfits. However, we did make love by the fire, several times, before falling asleep wrapped in each other's embrace, happy and content.

# CHAPTER 19

AFTER OUR AMAZING VALENTINE'S NIGHT, WE SPENT THE WEEKEND together lazing around his house. And by lazing, I mean making love many, many times. We finally got around to playing a game of Sexy Truth or Dare and we wore our outfits. It took a blow job to convince him to wear his briefs, but it was totally worth it. And I may have laughed and laughed when he stepped out of the bathroom in said briefs. He wasn't too happy with me over that, but all was forgiven when I slipped on my matching teddy, and as promised, I didn't wear anything else.

It's now Thursday, the day is dragging and I'm missing Bennett. The last time we saw each other was Monday night when we had dinner together after work. He's been tied up with a new project this week and it's been all hands on deck.

The elevator doors open and I step out into the lobby, glancing up, I see the building directory and grin when I see BKB's name, and then my mind drifts to my visit to his office on Monday evening…

*…I was on my way up to meet Bennett; we were going to grab a quick dinner at Lucio's. I'm addicted to the pasta there, especially the lasagna, the dish he served up on Valentine's Day, which he tried to pass off as his own handiwork. Even though we dine there often, I love the food and the atmosphere, but most of all, I get to see Lucio himself. He is the sweetest man ever, and boy, does he know how to cook.*

*Stepping into reception, Barb was on the phone but she waved to me and mouthed, 'Head on back.' Smiling, I walked down the hallway to his office; the door was ajar. I knocked as I pushed it open and stepped inside, Bennett was at his desk and when his eyes landed on mine, his face brightened.*

*"Is it that time already?"*

*Nodding my head, I walked around his desk and placed a quick kiss on his lips before leaning against the wood. He placed his hand on my thigh and ran his fingers up and down. Sliding his hand under my skirt, he spread my legs apart and rubbed my slit through my panties. Leaning back, I held my body weight on my arms and widened my legs. My eyes dropped closed and I moaned when he pushed the soaked material aside and rubbed my clit. "Bennett," I groaned. Opening my eyes, we stared at one another as he pushed a finger into me. My hips began to move against his hand, he slipped two more in and wriggled them around. Hitting all those sensitive magical spots. "I'm coming," I whisper-moaned. He pinched my nipple through my blouse and I came violently, my juices soaking his hand. I was sure I've left a mess on his desk. He pulled his hand out and lifted his fingers to his lips. Sliding them into his mouth, he sucked them clean.*

*Leaning forward, I slid my hand around his neck and pulled him to me. My mouth covered his for a searing hot kiss. I could taste myself on his lips and my clit pulsed to life again. Slipping off his desk, I pushed his chair back and dropped to my knees in front of him. Sliding under his desk, I ran my hands up his thighs like he just did to me. I made quick work of his button and zipper. Pulling his dick out, I stroked it with my eyes locked on his. My tongue darted out and I licked the tip, pre-ejaculate danced on my tongue.*

*Opening my mouth, I swallowed his cock down my throat, bobbing my head up and down. He leaned forward resting his palms on his desk. Our eyes locked on one another as I continued to swallow his cock. Taking it deeper and deeper each time.*

*"Benn, you got a minute?" Keeton said, stepping into Bennet's office. My eyes widened, but Bennett rolled his chair forward, trapping me under his desk.* Game on, *I thought to myself, and I increased the pressure of my sucks and began to massage his balls.*

*"Yeah," he groaned.*

*"Good, you're still here," Blair announced as he too walked in. "I thought we would have missed you."*

*"I'm still here," Bennett replied, his voice tight and high. I smiled with his dick still in my mouth, and I continued to suck and play with his balls. From above, I could hear them talking about a meeting next week. I wasn't really paying attention to them, I was focused on the cock sliding in and out of my mouth.*

*His body stiffened and I knew he was close. He was holding himself together quite well, but I wasn't done yet. Licking down the side of his cock, I sucked a ball into my mouth, and he was unable to hold in a groan.*

*"You all right?" one of the guys asked.*

*"Mmmhmpf, sore legs from the gym," he replied as I took his cock back into my mouth, sucking him like he was a melting ice-cream cone on a hot summer's day. Before long, his body stiffened and he exploded*

*in my mouth. I sucked every last drop and just as I popped his cock out, the guys were saying their goodbyes.*

*Bennett rolled back a little and glared down at me. I winked at him, but my face froze when I heard, Keeton say, "Nice shoes, Stacey."*

*My eyes popped wide open.*

*Bennett laughed.*

*Blair chided, "You dirty fucking dog."*

*Lifting my hand out, I waved at them both. "Bye, guys."*

*Bennett took my hand and helped me crawl out. Looking over the desk, I was relieved to see his office door was closed and it was now just the two of us. "You are a minx," Bennett said, as he helped me stand up. Wrapping his arms around my waist, he stared at me. His eyes filled with desire. "But you are my minx, and I wouldn't have you any other way."*

*"Good, 'cause this is how I am and I won't change for anyone."*

*"And that, is why I love you."*

*"I love you too, now take me to Lucio's, you are going to need sustenance for what I have in mind for later this evening."*

*"You have my attention, Ms. Thomms."*

*"And later, you'll have mine…naked…all night long."*

…As I step into the chilly night air with a grin on my face, feeling happy and content, I'm snapped back to the present by a clearing throat, and my moment of bliss deflates when I see who is standing before me.

# CHAPTER 20

"Amity," I tersely say, as I smile sweetly at Bennett's ex. But in my mind, I'm grabbing her head and smashing it into the wall beside us.

"You won't keep him," she snarls.

I look at her with a shocked expression on my face. "Excuse me?"

"You heard me. Once Bennett has had his fill of slumming it with a little receptionist whore like you, he'll come back to me. Just because you have sleepovers at his place, dinner out, and romantic strolls through Millennium Park, it doesn't mean shit when he's destined to be with me."

What the actual fuck?

Is this chick serious right now?

And how the hell does she know all of this?

Sighing, I look to the sky for strength to not bitch slap this shrew and making it worse for myself, and Bennett. Taking a deep breath, I shake my head. "Jealousy doesn't look good on you, Amity."

"It's not jealousy, bitch. It's the truth." She steps closer to me, I can smell the desperation seeping from her pores. "Enjoy him while you can."

Before I have a chance to reply, she spins on her heel and storms away from me. Shaking my head, I watch as she saunters away. I'm shocked at her outburst but at the same time, after the limited run-ins I've had with her, I'm not. A chill, and not from the cool February air, rushes over me when I think about the things she just revealed. A hand on my shoulder scares me half to death and I scream in shock.

"Shit, Stacey, I'm sorry. I didn't mean to scare you," Keeton says, his face etched with concern.

"It's fine," I say.

"Are you okay? You look concerned, and not just from me frightening you just now."

"Yeah. Nah, I'm fine." I don't want to tell him about this. I just want to forget it and move on, but at the same time, I want someone to confide in. However, that someone needs to not work closely with Bennett, because if he finds out, he'll lose his shit and I don't wish that upon anyone. I know I shouldn't, considering what a bitch she is, but I don't want to rock the boat. I smile and add, "Just off in la la land."

"Are you sure? You look spooked."

I shake my head. "No, no, I'm fine. Really."

"From my knowledge, when a woman says fine, she really isn't fine."

Biting my lip, I think, *What the hell*? He does have firsthand experience with her; maybe he can shed some light and offer me advice. "Amity just blindsided me and gave me a tongue-lashing."

"Fuck," he curses. "What shit did the she-devil spew?"

"To warn me Bennett will tire of me soon and come running back to her."

"That's never gonna happen. Hell will freeze over before he goes back to that bitch." He pauses. "You know she's full of shit, right?"

"Yeah, I know that." *Sort of.*

"But?"

"It's nothing. I'm not going to let her worry me. How are you? Seems like you guys are super swamped at the moment."

"Yeah, this project is bigger than any of us expected, but I think we are in the home stretch now."

"So how come you escaped the madhouse?"

"I'm on dinner duty."

"Lucky you."

"Not really. I have to go to three different places because we are three indecisive bastards when it comes to food."

A laugh escapes me. "If it was me, I'd get what I want since I had to leave the warmth of the office."

"I like your style, Stacey. Looks likes it's burgers for everyone then."

"Burgers sounds great. Mind if I tag along?"

"Sure…then I can blame you for the burgers."

"If it means I get to see Bennett, then blame away."

"You are just as smitten as he is. It's nice to see him smiling again."

We both start walking, I'm not sure where we are going but it's nice to be moving again, the air is quite chilly tonight. "Was she really that bad?"

"Badder then bad."

"Wow, from the limited interactions I've had with her, I don't see why he was with her."

"You and me both." We both laugh, "Shall we head to Rubies?"

"I haven't had a Ruby burger in ages."

"A girl after my own heart." He smiles and offers me his arm.

"Don't let Bennett hear you say that."

"I can handle him."

"I'm sure you can."

Linking my arm with his, we walk the few blocks to Rubies. It's pretty busy when we arrive, but we place our order and hang by the door. The food is ready much quicker than I expected, considering how busy it is, and with our burgers and fries in hand, we head back to the office.

Keeton and I are laughing as we step into reception. I follow him down the corridor toward the boardroom; he steps in first and says, "I come bearing burgers." Lifting the bags triumphantly in the air.

"Burgers, what the fuck, man?" Blair whines.

"Dude, I wanted sushi," Bennett cries.

"They come with a side of gorgeous girl," he offers, and I step out from behind him.

My eyes immediately find Bennett. "Hey," I quietly say, wondering if me being here is okay after all.

"Best dinner ever," Bennett says as he stands up. "Keet, you can be on dinner duty anytime."

He walks over to me, taking the food bag from my hand and places it on the table behind him. He turns his attention back to me. "Hey," he gruffly says, as he grips my cheeks and kisses me hello.

When we come back up for air, I grin. "Wow, that was some greeting."

"And now I'm no longer hungry," Blair teases. Bennett flips him the bird over his shoulder. His eyes are still firmly locked on me and I can feel his stare penetrating deep into my soul. With that one look, I forget all about Amity and her threat.

# CHAPTER 21
# BENNETT

"Let's eat," Keeton says, as he opens the bags dispersing the burgers and fries. Walking back to my chair, I sit down and smile when Stacey takes the seat beside me. Like always when she's near, I have to touch her. I place my hand on her thigh and gently squeeze. She glances down at my hand, then to back me. Her face lights up and she returns my smile. The air around us sizzles from that one look. My eyes are focused on her, everything and everyone else fades into the background. It's just her and me. A feeling of contentment washes over me. Love for this woman courses through my veins. Her angelic voice snaps me back to the present.

"Sorry, what?"

"I asked how this is all going?" Lifting her hand, she flicks her fingers toward the documents and files scattered on the table. "Keeton said you are slowly getting there, but this looks like a jumbled mess to me."

"Oddly, this mess is organized chaos." The three of us guys all laugh. "We are slowly getting there, but after this weekend, I think we'll have it all sorted." I look to her and hesitantly add, "I have to work through the weekend though."

"I guessed as much, but it's fine. I'm heading to Bin 501 with the girls tomorrow night anyway."

My body relaxes at her reply, I wasn't even aware of the tenseness in my shoulders until just now. I guess after being with Amity, I just expected an outburst or epic meltdown. Amity would have lost her shit at me not spending time with her on the weekend. Stacey's reaction right now is one of the many things I love about her. She gives us much as she takes, but most of all, she makes me a better person. She loves me for me, without needing or wanting anything in return.

"Sounds great. Maybe I can pick you up afterward and you can stay at my place?"

"As much as that sounds great, girls' night generally goes until the sun is coming up and you have a penis, therefore you are not invited."

"Dude, you just got cockblocked by your own cock," Blair laughs.

"Burn," Keeton adds.

Flipping them both the bird, I shake my head. "Immature dicks," I mumble, "Wow, you ladies go hardcore."

"You betcha we do. The last time we partied hard was when we were in Kansas for Kasey's bachelorette…" She drifts off and her eyes become glassy.

"Are you okay?" I ask, my hand cups her cheek and she looks to me. No longer is she happy and excited, she's sad, bordering on crying.

She shakes her head and wipes away a tear that escaped. "That was the weekend Kody died."

"Who's Kody?"

"He was Kasey fiancé."

"I thought Branson was her fiancé."

She sadly smiles. "He is. He's also Kody's brother."

My eyes bug out in surprise. "Let me get this straight. Kasey is engaged to Branson but she was engaged to Kody, who died. Who's the baby daddy? Or is this some incestuous love triangle thing?"

Blair and Keeton's heads pop up from their burgers and a look passes between them.

Stacey laughs. "No, no love triangle, just a sad yet romantic tale of love. Let me start at the beginning. Kasey was engaged to Kody, they were head over heels in love. We were in Kansas for her bachelorette party and while we were there, Kody was killed in a car accident. The day of his funeral, she found out she was pregnant. Branson, being the good brother he is, stepped up and helped Kasey. Along the way they fell in love. He delivered KJ and they got engaged on New Year's Eve and now they are living their happily ever after."

"Wow, that is quite the love story, but why were you in Kansas for her bachelorette party? Seems kinda random."

"To see a stripper named Jake," she says as she digs into her burger.

"You do know they have strip clubs here." She eyes me suspiciously. "So I've heard."

"Yeah, but Jake is in Kansas."

"How do you know this?"

"'Cause I'm awesome."

"That you are, Stacey Thomms, that you are."

The conversation turns to the weather and other random shit. We finish dinner and then it's time for Stacey to leave. "Back in a sec, guys. Just going to walk Stace out."

Blair leans into Keeton and with a playful wink toward Stacey and me and teases, "That's code for fuck her in reception."

My sassy girl flips him the bird. "You are just jealous 'cause you aren't getting any right now."

"Burn," Keeton says, and again a look passes between the two of them sparking my intrigue as to what's going on between them.

Everyone laughs...except for Blair who mumbles something about assholes under his breath.

"See you guys later," Stacey says, as she grabs her handbag.

"Later," Keeton says.

Blair waves, he's focused on the file in his hands right now but manages to say, "Laters, Babycakes."

Walking out, I rest my hand low on her back. My hand made its way there without me thinking about it. "Thanks for letting me crash dinner."

"You can crash anytime."

She presses the call button and looks to me. "I love you, Bennett."

"I love you too."

We step toward one another and press our lips together. This kiss is soft and passionate. The ding from the elevator pulls us apart. "Text me when you get home."

"Yes, Dad," she playfully replies, as she steps into the eleva-tor. She presses the button for the lobby and the doors begin to close. She lifts her hand to her lips and blows a kiss toward me. Smiling, I pretend to catch it and I press it to my heart. The last thing I see, before the doors close, is Stacey beaming back at me.

# CHAPTER 22

STEPPING OUT INTO THE COLD AIR, I SCOFF AT HOW COLD IT IS NOW. It was chilly when I left earlier, but now, it's freezing. Pulling my coat tightly around me, I head toward the "L" train, hoping I won't have to wait too long for one.

I'm crossing the street when the hairs on the back of my neck stand on end. Looking around, I don't see anything out of the ordinary but that prickly feeling is there with each step I take. As I continue to walk, that feeling won't go away and it's getting stronger and stronger. Not willing to risk my safety, I turn into the Starbucks and immediately the eerie feeling dissipates.

Walking to the counter, I order myself a coffee and while I wait, I book an Uber to take me home.

Ten minutes later, I'm in the back of an Uber and the panic I felt previously has vanished. We pull up to my place and I race inside. As I walk across the lobby, I tell myself the feeling was due to the cold but I don't believe it at all.

As soon as I step into my apartment, I let out the breath I didn't realize I was holding. With a sigh, I remove my coat and hang it up. Dropping my bag on the kitchen counter, I head into my bedroom. Grabbing my pajamas, I change into them. Then I head back to the kitchen and pour myself a glass of wine, grab my iPad, and snuggle on the loveseat. Grabbing my phone, I text Bennett, like I said I would, before I engross myself in Dean Koontz's latest release.

Waking a few hours later, my iPad is on my face and I'm still on the loveseat. Placing the device on my coffee table, I lie on the couch, pull the blanket Nanna Thomms crocheted for me up and over my body and drift back to sleep immediately, dreaming of Bennett and how happy he makes me.

The next morning, I ache all over—I'm too old to sleep on the loveseat anymore. Looking to the clock on the wall in the kitchen, I see it's nearly eleven. I haven't slept this late in ages. Stretching, I stand up and decide since I don't have to meet the girls 'til later, I'll have a bath to soak my aching body. Walking into my en suite bathroom, I turn on the faucets and begin to fill the bath. Pouring in some freesia and green tea bubble bath, the aroma instantly hits the air and I smile.

Racing into the kitchen, I pour myself a mimosa—hey, it's girls' night—and I head back into the bathroom. The water is high enough for me climb in. Submerging myself in the water, I moan and relax in the tub.

Grabbing my phone, I call decide to call Mom. It's been a

while since I've spoken to her. We don't get to chat long as she and Dad are heading out for the afternoon. I do update her on my relationship with Bennett. She's over the moon that I'm finally dating 'a good one,' as she put it. Saying our goodbyes, I hang up and sink into the tub.

My eyes drift closed as the water engulfs me. I feel my body loosen up. My limbs mold to the tub. Grabbing my drink, I take a sip and moan. This is just what I needed.

My phone pings with a text, picking it up, I smile when I see it's from Bennett.

**Bennett** *Morning, Gorgeous. Hope you slept well.*
**Stacey:** *Morning, Handsome. Fell asleep on the loveseat with Dean.*
**Bennett** *Who the fuck is Dean????*

A laugh escapes me at his reply.

**Stacey:** *Down boy, Dean Koontz. I was reading his latest and fell asleep. I'm too old to sleep on the couch, so I'm soaking in the tub right now.*
**Bennett** *Don't tell me that.*
**Stacey:** *Don't tell you that I'm all wet and soapy?*
**Stacey:** *...did I mention wet???*
**Bennett:** *Stacey.*

Deciding to be brazen, I strategically place the bubbles across my chest and take a sexy selfie and send it to him.

**Bennett:** *Stacey.*
**Bennett:** *You are a little minx.*
**Stacey:** *Maybe.*

**Bennett:** *I'm going to spank that fine ass of yours tomorrow night.*
**Stacey:** *Promises. Promises.*
**Bennett:** *Your ass is definitely mine.*
**Stacey:** *We've discussed this before, you ain't getting anywhere near my ass.*

My phone rings and I immediately answer, "Hey."

"Don't hey me, woman. My cock is harder than steel right now. Not only am I picturing your sexy ass in the tub, but I'm also picturing me shoving my cock into your sexy as sin ass—"

"Yeah, that's not gonna happen...ever...my ass is a one-way passage."

"We'll see about that."

"Yeah, nah, not gonna happen, buddy. Feel free to spank it, but your cock ain't ever going inside it."

"We will discuss this when I can punish you."

"Promise?"

"You bet your fine ass I promise."

"As I've told you, my ass is off limits." We both laugh, and then I add, "I love you, Bennett."

"Don't butter me up by saying I love you, and we will discuss your ass in great detail."

"Mmmhmpf."

He's silent and then adds, "I love you."

"I love you too."

We both go quiet, I move and the waters splashes. "Are you still in the bath?"

"Maybe."

"Fuck me," he groans.

"Tomorrow night I will," I playfully reply.

"Fuck," he groans again, "I'm going to go before I say fuck it and drive over to your place, so I can have my wicked way with you."

"I'm down with that plan," I teasingly add.

"Babe, if I could I would."

"Just think, in thirty-one hours' time, I'll be answering my door in nothing but my birthday suit, and you can have your wicked way with me."

"Seriously, woman, you are going to be the death of me."

"Sorry, but if it's any consolation, I'm super horny right now too."

"It helps…a little…but my dick is still rock-hard."

"As are my nipples."

"Fuck. I'm going to go now before I explode."

A laugh escapes me. "Okay, I'll behave now. See you tomorrow night."

"Yes, you will, and I really hope you answer the door how you promised."

"I promise."

We hang up and I sink back into the tub, with a grin on my face and a throbbing clit.

Strolling into Bin 501 later that afternoon, I feel alive and I cannot wait for the night ahead. As soon as I step inside, I see the girls at 'our' high-top table. Strutting over to them, Kasey spots me first and she wolf-whistles at me. Marlee, turns and smiles, "Work it girl," she shouts, as she sips on a mocktail since she's knocked up and as a bonus, we have a designated driver for the next nine months.

I'm a few mimosas in, so I spin around and shake my booty as I strut my stuff over to the girls. Hellos and kisses are shared before a glass of wine is thrust into my hand from Kasey. Her cheeks are flushed and her eyes glassy, looks like she's had a few already too.

A few hours later, the table is littered with empty wine glasses and we are laughing like hyenas. This was just what I needed. "You know," I say, as I look between my three friends, "I love you ladies hard. I'm so glad to have met you all and—"

"Ohh no, here comes drunk emotional, Stacey," Kasey says with a big goofy grin on her face.

"Whatever, bitch. As I was saying, I love you guys. I'm glad to have met you all, and I'm even more gladder that even though you all have cute little babies or a bun in the oven," I reach over and rub Marlee's tummy, "that you still have time for no baby me."

"You are stuck with us," Chelle declares. "And from what I've heard, you will be joining the baby wagon one of these days soon."

"I may be blissfully in love, but no babies for now. I want to enjoy the spontaneous out of this world sexy times while we can."

"Who says you can't do that with a child?" Kasey offers, "Just the other day—"

Kasey is cut off mid-sentence, "Ohh look, it's Bennett's whore and her skanks."

Spinning around, I come face-to-face with Amity. "Amity," I grate between clenched teeth.

"You really have no shame, don't you?"

"Excuse me?"

"You are out, whoring yourself with your posse, meanwhile Bennett is slaving away at the office."

"I beg your pardon?"

"You heard me, bitch," she says, stepping toward me.

"I'm not the bitch here, Amity. It's no wonder Bennett dumped your sorry ass."

"He'll come back to me. I'll make sure he will."

"You really think he's going to take back a cheating whore like you? You really are delusional, Amity."

Before I register what's happening, Amity pulls her hand back and slaps me across the face. My eyes pop open in shock, but before I can say anything, Branson and one of the bouncers are dragging a screaming Amity away from us, escorting her from the premises. Lifting my hand to my cheek, I cup it. The skin burning from the contact. I've never been bitch-slapped before and can't say I ever want to again.

"Who the hell was that?" Marlee asks, as she slides her arm around me, pulling me into her side for a hug.

"Bennett's ex," I offer, as I rub my tingling cheek.

"She seems…umm, ahh, unhinged," Marlee says.

"Yep." I nod. "Would you believe this isn't the first run-in I've had with Amity?"

"What?" the three of them scream together. My ear ringing from Marlee's screech right beside me.

The three of them stare at me. "I need more wine for this." Chelle refills my glass…to the top, and then she looks at me in a 'okay, now explain yourself' kind of way.

Taking a sip, and by sip, I mean huge gulp, I swallow the fruity elixir and take a deep breath. Then I proceeded to tell the girls all about Amity Cuthell. When I'm finished, the three of them sit there silently, mouths open in shock, and stare at me.

Kasey is the first to speak, "Ummm, why are we only hearing about Whoreity and her whoreness now?"

"Because she isn't worth it," I nonchalantly reply, because she isn't. I'm not going to let her get to me, otherwise, she wins and I refuse to let her win.

"Stace, Whoreity has verbally attacked you multiple times now AND tonight, she physically assaulted you. You really should press charges."

"NO!" I scream. "I just want to forget about it and move on. Like seriously, what's she going to do? Scratch my eyeballs out with her cat-like claws?"

"Probably," Kasey says. "That woman has an obsession with Bennett, and right now Stace, you are the center of his universe, and with that, you are also at the center of her obsession." She pauses. "What does Bennett think of all this?"

"He was there for the first verbal tirade, but he doesn't know about yesterday, or just now."

"Stacey," Kasey chastises me. She reaches across the table to squeezes my hand. "You need to tell him about this."

"I don't want to worry him, he's so busy with work and when we are together, I don't want to talk about her."

"Maybe he can talk with her."

"No, I don't want him anywhere near, what did you call her, Whoreity. If I just leave it be, she will go away when she realizes we aren't giving in."

"I don't think that's the right course of action, but I trust you," Kasey says.

The rest of the night isn't as joyous and fun as before Amity's arrival, but the four of us have a great night, just like we always do.

# CHAPTER 23

WAKING WITH AN EPIC HANGOVER, I DON'T DO MUCH BECAUSE EACH time I move, or open my eyes, I feel like I'm dying. I text the girls to let them know I hate them and I'm barely alive; the bitches all laugh at me. I also texted Bennett several times, reconfirming we are still on for tonight.

Finally, I crawl out of bed, but I don't feel up to doing much. So I laze on the sofa and binge watch *Supernatural*, while eating my weight in pepperoni pizza and drinking gallons of Diet Coke.

Late in the afternoon, I receive a text from Bennett.

**Bennett -** *Leaving the office now. Heading home to shower and then I'll be over.*
**Stacey -** *Can't wait to see you.*

Climbing off the couch, I quickly tidy up and race into the bathroom for a shower. The hot water soothes my body, and when I step out, I feel refreshed and no sign of my hangover is present anymore.

Grabbing my moisturizer, I lather my body from head to toe then I slip on my robe while I fix my hair. Not wanting to have to blow-dry and straighten it, I spritz on some salt spray and grab a butterfly clip to messily put it up. Looking at my reflection in the mirror, I smile. For once my hair looks amazing like this, rather than its usual bird's nest.

I've just swiped on some gloss when my phone pings with a text.

**UNKNOWN -** *Won't be long.*

Shrugging my shoulders, I scrunch my face in confusion. This is the third time I have received this message, clearly someone has the wrong number. I throw it back on the bed when it beeps again

**Bennett -** *Just leaving now. Be there soon. X*

A smile graces my face as I read his text. Slipping on my sky high, black strappy heels, I walk into the kitchen and pour myself a glass of wine. The first mouthful is rough to swallow, damn girls and last night, but the second and third go down much smoother.

I've finished my glass of wine when there's a knock at my

door. With a grin, I take a deep breath and head to the door. Checking the peep hole, my grin widens when I see it's Bennett. Shrugging off my robe, it flits to the floor and I swing the door open, stepping back as I do as I don't want to give my neighbors a fright.

Bennett's eyes pop wide open before they roam over my body. My naked body, except for my shoes. The trail of his gaze sets my skin ablaze. Finally his eyes land on mine, "Well, are you going to come in?"

"Hell yes," he says, he steps inside, kicking the door shut behind him.

Turning on my heel, I walk into my apartment. Strutting my stuff as I walk away from him, I swish my hips side to side with each step I take. Glancing over my shoulder, I notice he's standing there, watching me intently.

Spinning to face him, I walk backward, raising my eyebrows seductively as I beckon him forward with my finger. Stopping just before my coffee table, my eyes are locked on him, and I watch as he starts toward me. I grin sheepishly. His eyes are filled with hunger, mirroring mine. Bennett and I have always had a connection, but right in this moment—me naked, him fully clothed—that connection is palpable. The air around us sizzling.

Lifting my hand, I graze my finger down my neck, between the valley of my breasts. Circling my navel before sliding down farther. Suddenly, Bennett is gripping my wrist, "Uh ah, that's mine."

"Really?" I playfully reply, as I pull my hand free and perch myself on the edge of my coffee table. Spreading my legs wide, I slide my finger down my groin, on the upward motion, I slide it between my lips. The pad of my finger brushes my clit, and I moan. Leaning back on my other arm, with my eyes locked on Bennett, I slide my finger up and down my slit.

Bennett drops to his knees before me. With his eyes locked on mine, he leans forward and inhales. "I love the smell of your pussy, but I love its taste even more." His tongue darts out and he licks between my lips, fastening his mouth on my swollen clit he sucks.

"Bennett," I moan, as he continues to devour me.

Leaning back on both my arms, I close my eyes and drop my head back, giving myself over to the pleasure building. He grips my hips and continues to lick and suck my vagina. He slips a finger inside me and I explode around him, my arousal soaking his face. Gripping his head with my thighs, I push him farther into me as I ride out my orgasm.

Collapsing back onto the coffee table, I lie there panting as my body comes back to earth and my breathing returns to normal. Suddenly, I'm floating. I'm in Bennett's arms and he carries me into the bedroom where we make love for the rest of the night.

Blissfully, we fall asleep in the wee hours of the morning, but the next day that bliss implodes in our face.

# CHAPTER 24
# BENNETT

SITTING AT MY DESK, I PLAY THE SCENES FROM LAST NIGHT OVER AND over in my head. Stacey and I have always had a connection, but last night it was off the charts. When I arrived and she was buck naked, I couldn't believe my eyes. Then after I carried her into bed, we made love for hours and hours. It was beyond perfect.

The ringing of my office line snaps me back to the present, which is a good thing because right now, my cock is harder than stone.

"Bennett Burnsteen."

"Bennett?" they question, I can't quite place the voice. "Baby?"

When they say baby, I know exactly who it is. "Amity, what do you want? I'm busy."

"I…"

"Spit it out woman, I don't have all day."

"Why are you so aggressive? She's causing you to be like this. Baby, she's changing you."

"SHE isn't doing anything to me, Amity. Apart from making me happier than I have ever been before, she has done nothing to me. I can't say the same for you."

"You and I belong together…"

"No!" I shout. "We don't. You had your chance, but you blew that when you slept with someone else. Listen, I've tried to be nice, but not anymore. You are no longer a part of my life. We are over. Dead and buried over. I've moved on, you moved on too, remember?"

"I left him," she quietly says.

"I don't give a flying fuck. Now, if you excuse me, I have work to do."

Slamming the phone down, I lean back in my chair and sigh in frustration. The happiness I felt just moments ago is gone, but I don't have time to dwell because Keeton walks in and sits in the chair across from me. He looks at me, and he immediately knows something is wrong. "What's up?"

"Amity."

"What the bitch do now? She accost Stacey again?"

My eyes snap to his. "What do you mean *again*?"

Keet's eyes pop wide open when he realizes I know nothing of Amity approaching Stacey.

"Spill now, before I lose my shit," I growl and lean toward him.

"Calm your shit, dude. Amity blindsided Stacey the night we came back with burgers."

"The fuck? Why didn't you tell me?"

"I thought she would have told you."

"Well, you thought wrong," I snarl, while he holds his hands up in defeat.

Picking up my phone, I dial her number and she picks up on the second ring. "Hey, handsome."

"Don't handsome me. Why didn't you tell me?" I snap, my voice full of anger and frustration.

"Tell you what?"

"About Amity."

"I didn't think it was an issue. The girls were with me—"

"The girls were with you when you left on Friday?"

"No, they were with me on Saturday."

"How many times have you had a run-in with Amity?"

"Ummm, three times."

"Three times!" I yell. "Why didn't you tell me?"

"'Cause there's nothing to tell. She's just jealous that you've moved on, and besides, I'm a big girl, I can handle chicks like Amity."

"Stacey, I know you are, but I need to know you are safe. I want you to be safe. When and where have you seen Amity?"

"Your office that day. Outside on Friday, and on Saturday night with the girls at Bin 501." She pauses. "What's going on?"

"Nothing, I just hate that my past is having an impact on you."

"Bennett, I'm fine. Really. She's nothing to worry about, I'm not worried and you shouldn't be either."

"You really are something, Stacey Thomms."

"I know," she says. "How about dinner at my place tonight?"

"Sounds perfect, I'll swing by and pick you up after five, we can head to your place together."

"Sounds like a plan and, Bennett?"

"Yeah."

"I love you."

"Love you too."

We hang up, and after talking with Stacey, I realize she's right, there's no need to worry about Amity. Soon enough, she'll find some other schmuck to attach herself to, and then she'll forget all about me. She's in my past and there's nothing she can do that will make me ever go back to her, not when I have someone as amazing as Stacey Thomms in my life.

# CHAPTER 25

LACING MY FINGERS WITH BENNETT'S, WE HEAD UP TO MY PLACE after parking in the garage below my building. We stopped at Jewell Osco, and I grabbed what I need to make us steak and steamed veggies with my famous creamy garlic mushroom sauce. We step out of the elevator, and when we get to my door, we notice it's ajar.

"That's weird, my cleaner must not have closed it properly when she left today."

Pushing the door open, I take a step inside. Dropping my bag at my feet, I freeze as my eyes dart around my apartment. "My

God," I say, lifting my hand to my mouth in shock. The scene before me is utter chaos. My apartment has been trashed. My loveseat has been tipped over, the cushions torn. My barstools have been thrown across the room. It looks like every item I own has been picked up, tossed across the room, and smashed.

Dropping to my knees, I shake my head. Bennett crouches next to me and when he places his hand on my thigh and squeezes, the flood gates open and I begin to cry. "Bennett, w-w-who would d-d-d-do this?" But as soon as I say it, I know. "Amity," I whisper.

"Let's not jump to conclusions," he says, my head snaps to his.

"Are you shitting me right now? There's no one else it could be."

Standing up, I turn my back to him and walk over to where I dropped my handbag. Bending down, I pick it up and pull my phone out and call the police. Holding the phone between my ear and shoulder, I lift one of my barstools upright and take a seat. Leaning forward, I rest my elbow on the countertop and massage my forehead, while holding the phone to my ear with the other.

Hanging up, I notice that Bennett has poured me a glass of water. "Thanks," I quietly say as I bring the glass to my lips. The silence between Bennett and I is deafening. "Who do you think did this?" he asks, breaking the silence.

Raising my eyebrows, I shake my head. "Really? You still are maintaining that this," I flick my hand around the room, "isn't Amity's doing?"

"No, I don't think she did this. Yes, she's a bitch, but she's not a destructive person, she wouldn't do this."

"Bennett, this was personal. If it was a normal break-in, they would not have trashed everything I own." I pause and stare at him. "This was personal and it was Amity."

"You don't know that."

"Bennett!" I yell. "It was her. I feel it in my bones."

Before we can fight any further, two officers enter my apartment.

A few hours later, we've given our statements and forensics have taken a fingerprint they found on the upturned coffee table. Bennett says I can stay at his place, but I'm too tired and emotional to fight, so I pack a bag and go with him. We don't say a word to one another on the ride back to his place, and for the first time ever, we don't drift off to sleep wrapped in each other's arms.

Waking the next morning, I reach out to Bennett but all I feel is a cold sheet beneath my hand. Rolling to my side, I absently stare at the wall. The events of yesterday come crashing back to me and I cry. Once I've let it all out, I hop out of bed, walk into his kitchen, and hope we can sort this out. Stepping into the room, I see it's empty, and I don't feel his presence like I usually do. He left for work without saying goodbye to me, that cuts more than him not believing me about Amity.

Shaking my head, I walk back into his room, shower, and change for work. Ordering an Uber, I step outside to wait for it. While I'm waiting the feeling of being watched washes over me, but thankfully, my Uber pulls up and I climb in.

Traffic is light and I make it to the office in plenty of time to grab a coffee before I start. I'm in line when someone taps me on the shoulder, I jump in fright and when I turn around I see Blair and Keeton standing there together.

"Shit, you scared the utter crap out of me."

"Sorry, you were off in la la land. I've been saying your name for like five minutes," Blair says.

"Five minutes? Really?"

"I may have exaggerated that a little."

"Just a little?"

We are at the front of the line and Keeton orders his and Blair's coffees and then looks to me. "I'll have an extra-large, skinny caramel latte please."

Keeton pays and we step to the end counter and wait for our drinks.

"Where's loverboy?" Blair asks.

Shrugging my shoulders. "Work probably."

"Ohh oh, trouble in paradise."

"You could say that."

"What's up?" Blair asks.

"My apartment was broken into yesterday ,and when I told the officers I thought it might have been Amity, he defended her."

"The fuck?" Blair says, while Keeton says, "What the hell?"

"We got into a big fight, and then when I woke this morning, he'd already left."

"That was a dick thing to do," Keeton says, "but Bennett loves you, Stacey. How would you feel if an ex did that to Bennett? You wouldn't want to think that someone you were with could do something so sinister like that. Sure, we all know she's a psycho bitch-faced troll, but Bennett—at one point— loved her unconditionally."

"I guess you're right."

With our coffees in hand, the three of us walk to the office. I get off on my floor and say bye to the guys. As I sit down at my desk, I mull over what Keeton said, *How would I feel if one of my exes did this? Would I defend them like Bennett did with Amity?* I've just turned my computer on when my phone pings with a text.

**Bennett:** *I'm sorry.*
**Bennett:** *I love you.*
**Bennett:** *Please don't hate me.*
**Stacey:** *I don't hate you. I love you too, but you…*
**Bennett:** *What?*
**Stacey:** *You pissed me off defending her…it hurt's that you don't believe me.*
**Bennett:** *I'm sorry.*
**Bennett:** *I just can't believe she'd do this. Sure she's a spiteful bitch, but she wouldn't stoop this low.*
**Stacey:** *I have to work. We can argue later.*
**Bennett:** *I don't want to argue with you.*
**Stacey:** *I don't either.*

The stairwell door flies open, I jump in fright and drop my phone. An enraged Amity steps into reception and storms over to me. Her face is full of rage. Her eyes are wild with fury, all directed at me.

"I have just had a visit from the police, you bitch. How dare you accuse me of trashing your apartment?" she screams, spit flying from her mouth.

"Amity, your fingerprints were found in my apartment."

"You know he'll leave you. He left me—"

"Because you cheated," I throw back at her.

"Potato. Partato." She shakes her head. She smiles at me but from the vengeful look in her eyes, it's sinister. "You've ruined everything, you know." She looks at me, her eyes black with anger. "I want you to suffer like I'm suffering right now." She pulls a gun from her purse and points it at me. "I want you gone, so Bennett and I can get back to being happy."

From the corner of my eye, I see Gage in the hallway; he has his phone to his ear. He makes a move to step into reception but

I shake my head. Amity sees my movement and goes to turn toward Gage.

Lifting my hands in defeat, I shake my head faster and faster. "Please, Amity," I beg, "we can work this out."

"There's only one way for this to go."

"Anything, I'll do anything."

"Leave and never come back. Forget you ever met Bennett Burnsteen. Let Benny and I have the life together."

I know that to save myself, and everyone in this office, I need to play along with this psycho bitch. A tear leaks from my eye. "Do you promise to look after him?"

"With my life."

Nodding my head, I smile at her. "Fine. You win." Quietly I add, "He's all yours."

"I knew you didn't love him. You gave up too easily."

"Yep, you got me, Amity. I never loved him, I was just using him."

"You are such a bitch. How could you do that to a man like Bennett? He's everything."

Another tear cascades down my cheek. "Yep."

Stepping around the desk, Amity freezes, "What are you doing?"

"Leaving like you want me too."

She flicks her hand holding the gun toward to elevator. "Off you go then." She leans forward and presses the call button. Slowly I walk toward her and the elevator doors open. Bennett steps into reception. His eyes pop open at the scene before him.

"Benny, baby," she singsongs. Lowering the gun, she gazes at Bennett, and I take the chance to strike, but she's quicker than I give her credit for. She raises the gun and fires. A burning feeling shatters through my shoulder.

"Stacey!" Bennett shouts.

"Benny!" Amity yells.

My body hits the reception floor with a thud. Everything around me blurs. My hearing is muffled. Someone rolls me to my back. "Stacey, baby, stay with me."

Bennett's face comes into view, and then suddenly darkness takes over and I slip into the black abyss.

# CHAPTER 26

BLINKING MY EYES A FEW TIMES, THEY FINALLY OPEN AND STAY OPEN. My vision clears and the room comes into focus. My mind is fuzzy and I'm confused as to where I am. The walls are stark white. The bed is uncomfortable and there's an incessant beeping from a machine beside me. That's when I realize I'm in a hospital bed. Looking down, I see I'm in a hospital gown and there's a bandage covering my left shoulder and upper arm. Trying to sit up, I wince in agony; letting out a groan as a searing hot pain shoots through my shoulder and down my arm.

"Take it easy, baby," Bennett says, as he jumps up and comes toward me. I notice his face is pale and etched with worry.

He freezes and we stare at each other. "Hey," we both say at the same time, each of us grinning at our in sync hello. As I'm staring at him, it hits me that this is the most we've spoken to one another in the last twelve hours.

"What happened?" I ask, as the events are a little unclear in my mind.

"What do you remember?"

"I remember waking up alone. Going to the office, texting you." Then I pause and my mind replays the events at the office before my eyes in vivid color and detail. My right hand gently rubs over the gunshot wound that's currently throbbing.

"She shot me," I whisper, looking to Bennett my eyes well with tears. "Bennett," I whine, as worry courses through my veins that she's going to come back and finish what she started.

"You're safe," he says, as if he can read my mind, "Amity is in prison. She has been charged with breaking and entering, attempted murder, and resisting arrest."

My eyes pop open at that last charge. "Resisting arrest?"

"Yeah, she lost her shit with the arresting officer. Gage tells me the officer ended up with a black eye, hence an additional charge for assaulting an officer."

"Wow, she's more psycho than I thought." Licking my lips, I then ask, "Was anyone else hurt?"

He shakes his head from side to side. "You are the only person I know who, with a gunshot wound, is worried about others." He lifts my hand to his lips and presses a kiss to my knuckles.

"Was anyone else hurt?" I ask again.

"No, just you and the officer who was hit." He takes a seat on the mattress next to me, his eyes are locked on mine. They drop to my shoulder and he leans forward and rests his head on my stomach and hugs me. "Baby, I'm so sorry I didn't believe you," he cries. "I knew she was crazy, but I didn't realize the extent of her insanity."

My hand lifts on its own accord and I run my fingers through his hair in a soothing manner. "Bennett, look at me?" I whisper. He lifts his gaze to mine and I smile at him. "I'm fine, and none of us could have known how unhinged she was."

"You got shot because of me."

"No, I got shot because of her." I cup his face in my palm, he leans into it and a gently run my finger along his jawline. It's scruffy against the pad of my thumb. "Bennett, I'm sorry for—"

"No, you don't need to say sorry to me. I'm the one who will spend the rest of my life being sorry for what happened." His gaze drops to my shoulder, "Your skin will be marred forever because of me."

"Her," I interrupt.

"Because of her, and I promise, you will never be in a situation like that again."

Before I can reply, the door to my room bursts open. Mom and Dad step into the room. As soon as my eyes land on Mom; I begin to cry. "Mom," I blubber, she races over to the bed and shoves Bennett out of the way. She sits on the bed next to me and cups my face like I was just holding Bennett's.

Her eyes drop to my bandaged shoulder, "Ohh, my baby girl," she cries. "Don't ever scare me like that again."

"I'm sorry, Mom."

"And, you," Mom snarls looking at Bennett, "How could you let this happen to my baby?"

"Mrs. Thomms—" Bennet says, but Mom raises her hand halting him, she stands up to stare at him.

"I'm not finished." Dad and I smirk at each other. "You need to take better care of my daughter. I don't ever want to get a call like that again." She pauses and then adds, "Now come give me a hug, I want to get a closer look at the man who's won over my daughter's heart."

Bennett steps to Mom and she grips his cheeks, inspecting him. She nods and then wraps her arms around his waist. She rests her head on his chest since she's five foot nothing compared to his six plus feet. He hugs her back, seeing them like that sparks something inside of me and I begin to cry again.

"Stacey, honey, why are you crying?" Dad asks.

"I'm happy," I wail, as tears continue to pour down my cheeks.

"You have a funny way of showing your happiness, honey."

"Well, when you get shot you can show your happiness however you want."

"She'll be fine." Mom says, winking at Bennett. "The sass is back, hope you can handle it, young man."

"I'm sure I'll be fine."

He looks to me, and I know with that one look, Bennett and I will be just fine.

# CHAPTER 27

*...Three weeks later*
*...March 23rd, 2020*

TODAY IS MY FIRST DAY BACK AT WORK. THE LAST THREE WEEKS HAVE been tough, to say the least, but throughout it all, Bennett was by my side. He managed to get my apartment sorted while I was in the hospital, but I haven't spent much time there. I've spent every night at Bennett's, and I have to say, waking up beside Bennett each and every morning is pretty spectacular.

The elevator dings and out steps, you guessed it, the delivery shit. "Sign here please," he snarls and I eye him.

"Really?"

"This one IS actually for WFOX-FM and it's addressed to: The sexiest receptionist at WFOX-FM."

"Give me that, it does not," I snap, but when my eyes drop to the signature board, it says those exact words.

"Fine," I huff, and I scribble my signature on the line and take the box from him. He winks at me before he walks back to the elevators.

Stepping back behind the desk, I take a seat. I'm just about to open my unexpected package when the phone rings. Clicking the button on my headset, I answer, "Welcome to WFOX-FM, this is Stacey."

"Is this Stacey, the sexiest receptionist at WFOX-FM?"

"It sure is," I laugh. "Am I speaking with the sweetest and sexiest owner of BKB Incorporated?"

He laughs down the phone and my face breaks out in a smile. The last few weeks have been rough for Bennett, he's harboring guilt and holding himself responsible for what happened to me. I've tried to tell him a million times that he's not responsible for Amity's actions, but he's a stubborn bastard and won't listen to me.

"Ohh, you think I'm sexy?" he croons into my ear.

"Is your ego in need of stroking?" I ask.

"No, but something else could do with some stroking."

"Really? The quickie in the parking lot, not ninety-three minutes ago, wasn't enough."

"It will never be enough when it comes to sinking myself inside you, Stacey Thomms."

"Ohh, Bennett, you have such a way with words."

"Have you opened your package yet?"

"No, some sexy horny bastard called and interrupted me."

"Well have at it, Ms. Thomms."

"Why thank you, Mr. Burnsteen."

Picking up the box, I pull the knot of the bow and it falls open. Lifting the lid off, I stare at a key ring. "A key ring?" I ask.

"Read the note under the lid." He pauses. "Out loud."

"Okay." Lifting up the lid, I see Bennett's beautiful penmanship and I smile. "Stacey Thomms, will you do me the honor of accepting this key ring and move in with me?" Covering my mouth, my eyes well with tears.

"Are you crying?" he asks, I totally forgot I was on the phone with him.

"You know I cry when I'm happy, and yes, yes, I'll..." but I don't get to finish what I'm saying because the stairwell door swings open and Bennett steps in. Standing up, I race over to him, throw my arms around his neck, and slam my lips against his.

He pulls back. "There is one condition of you moving in with me."

"Just one?"

"Yeah, and this is pretty major."

"Oooookay," I hesitantly say. "Hit me with your one major condition."

"You have to move in as my wife."

I freeze.

My eyes bug wide open.

I blink several times as I process his condition.

"Say that again?" I manage to spit out once my brain catches up.

"You can only move in permanently, if you are my wife." Opening my mouth to speak, he places his finger over my lips. "Me and you leave here tonight, then we jump on a plane, fly to Vegas, get hitched, and when we return, you move in."

"Are you serious?"

"Deadly. Stacey, you are my everything and I don't want to waste another minute not being married to you."

"Yes!" I shout. "Yes, I'll marry you and move in with you. I want everything with you, Bennett. You ARE my everything and I cannot wait to become Mrs. Everything to your Mr. Everything."

And that's what we did, we finished out our workday, and then we jumped on a plane, flew to Las Vegas, and at the *Chapel of the Flowers* I became Mrs. Stacey Burnsteen. This was an unexpected proposal but it was perfect in every way. I now get to spend the rest of my life with this man, and I've finally got what all my friends have, my very own happily ever after.

# EPILOGUE

*...December 12th, 2020*

I'M SITTING AT MY DESK AND THE ELEVATOR DOORS OPEN, A FAMILIAR delivery shithead steps out. He shrugs his shoulders at me, and like he has done on a monthly basis since I discovered Bennett's trickery, he says the same three words, "Sign here, please."

December twelfth, 2019 was the day everything changed for me. One unexpected package—thank you, Stephen King—changed the course of my life; it led me to Bennett Burnsteen. With everything that he and I have been through, I wouldn't change a thing, not even getting shot.

As fate would have it, I have a package with two pink lines I want to share with my husband...and this delivery shithead is going to help me deliver one package I know will be completely unexpected for my husband.

**THE END!!!**

Read on for a sneak peek at The Unexpected Connection, book 4 in the Unexpected series.

## CHAPTER - FAITH

Flipping my head up, I shake my locks and stare at my reflection in the mirror. My lips lift into a grin, this color is off the charts bright, my parents, especially prim and proper mom, would have a conniption if they could see me now. No longer do I wear pearls and pant suits. No longer is my hair coiled into a quiff and stiff with a heap of hairspray. No longer do I watch the clock, making sure I'm where I need to be, when I need to be. Now? Now my life is free of rules and timetables. My hair is mine to do as I please. For the first time in twenty-two years, I march to the beat of my own drum. I've never been happier... and I'm never going back.

Tonight, I'm heading to a new club that's opened up, Tingle, with my room mate Ella Jennings. As soon as I met Ella, I knew I'd found my new best friend. From the moment we met, we clicked on every level and soon, she *was* my best friend and room mate. She made the whole getting away from my family thing so much easier.

My parents, Fleur and Arnold Robinson-Bailey, are what you call stuck up assholes. They think they are better than everyone and people bow down to them. My mother is the mayor and my father is a top notch lawyer. People in Collinsville think the sun shines out of their ass, what they don't realize is that behind closed doors they are two very different people. Me escaping their clutches was a long arduous process, that took months of scheming and plotting. I've been gone for six months now and I'm surprised they haven't come looking for me. Then again, I told them I was traveling through Europe to study the arts. That appeased mother, I don't think father gave a crap, as long as he has his Scotch and his secretaries, he's a happy man. Instead, I headed to Chicago, found Ella and the new me.

The only thing I miss about home is the warm weather. In Florida cold days are few and far between; here its cold for weeks, no months at a time but at least I can rock kick ass boots and the coats are to die for—I now have a coat addiction, hey its better than a coke addiction. I have one for each and every occasion; that's the only piece of advice from mother that I have adhered to; *"You must have something unique for all occasions."*

Ella steps into my bedroom and whistles pulling me from my memories and back into the present. "Holy hotness woman. If I batted for the same team, I'd totally do you." Looking down, I smile. I'm wearing a mini silver strapless dress that hugs my body and doesn't leave much to the imagination. On my feet are a pair of sky high ankle boots but it's my new hair that I love most. The color is intense and makes my eyes pop. I've left it wavy tonight and my make up light.

"Says the hot one." Ella is wearing leather pants with a bright pink boob tube top and sky high matte black heels that elongate her killer calves.

"We are totally hooking up tonight."

"Ohh, yes please. I need a good fuck and an amazing orgasm."

"You and me both sista."

"Then let's do it."

We grab our clutches and head to Tingle…for a night that I will never forget.

The Unexpected Connection is out now.

# ACKNOWLEDGMENTS

You'd think after thirteen books that these would get easier but as time has gone on, my team has expanded and there's more and more people to thank...and as usual, I always forget someone...sorry if I forgot you know that I do still love you.

Thank you to my editor, **Karen** from **Barren Acres Editing;** you worked on this book in Canada while you were on vacation (or holidays as we say here in Australia). I'm not jealous at all that my book was in Canada while I was not.

Thank you so much to **Dana Leah** from **Designs by Dana**. I know I'm picking but thank you for a stunning cover. I didn't give you much to work with but you worked your magic and you captured Stacey and Bennett perfectly.

As usual, a shout out to my beta babes; **Alley, Cherie, Halle** and **Jenny** . Without you guys, this would be a big old mess. Thanks for your feedback, guidance and support.

Thank you to **Ena** and **Amanda** from **Enticing Journey**. It's a pleasure working with you ladies. You made the release of this series so easy. I look forward to working with you ladies again.

Thanks to my hubby, **Troy** and my munchkins, **Piper** and **Kade**. You three are my everything. You make this authoring journey that much easier. Your support and hugs are everything. Love you guys long-time Xo

And lastly, as always, **you, my reader**. Without you guys, I wouldn't continue to do this. Your messages and reviews mean the world to me. From the bottom of my heart, thank you.

Wine Not (Book 3)

The Final Shot (Book 4)

The Liquor Cabinet: Series boxset

---

**STAND ALONES**

Out of Nowhere

Antecedent

Seven Nights

Falling for Dr. Kelly, a Falling novel

Falling for Dr. Knight, a Falling novel - coming May 2020

Doc Steel - coming June 2020

The Dirty Dozen: Alpha edition

The Rule Breaker Anthology - coming soon

In the Dark of Night anthology (only available in paperback directly from me)

Titanic Tales, a charity anthology (no longer available)

Gone Coastal, a sizzling summer beach anthology (no longer available)

Leave Me Breathless: The Lilac Collection (no longer available)

# ABOUT THE AUTHOR

 DL Gallie is from Queensland, Australia, but she's lived in many different places all over the world, including the UK and Canada. She currently resides in Central Queensland with her husband and two munchkins. She and her husband have been together since she was sixteen, and although they drive each other crazy at times, she couldn't imagine her life without him.

Shortly after her son was born, DL began reading again. With encouragement from her husband, she picked up the pen and started writing, and now the voices in her head won't shut up.

DL enjoys listening to music, drinking white wine in the summer, red wine in the winter, and beer all year round. She's also never been known to turn down a cocktail, especially a margarita.